D0345482

Also by Chuck Palahniuk

Fight Club

Survivor

Invisible Monsters

Choke

Lullaby

Fugitives and Refugees

Diary

Stranger Than Fiction

Haunted

Rant

Snuff

Pygmy

CHUCK PALAHNIUK

Tell-All

Doubleday

New York London Toronto
Sydney Auckland

ⅅ
DOUBLEDAY

Copyright © 2010 by Chuck Palahniuk

All rights reserved. Published in the United States by Doubleday, a division of Random House, Inc., New York.

www.doubleday.com

DOUBLEDAY and the DD colophon are registered trademarks of Random House, Inc.

Book design by Michael Collica

Library of Congress Cataloging-in-Publication Data
Palahniuk, Chuck.
Tell-all / Chuck Palahniuk. — 1st ed.
p. cm.
1. Hollywood (Los Angeles, Calif.)—Fiction. I. Title.
PS3566.A4554T45 2010
813'.54—dc22
2009032846

ISBN 978-0-385-52635-7

PRINTED IN THE UNITED STATES OF AMERICA

1 3 5 7 9 10 8 6 4 2

First Edition

To E.A.H.

Boy meets girl.

Boy gets girl.

Boy *kills* girl?

ACT I, SCENE ONE

Act one, scene one opens with **Lillian Hellman** clawing her way, stumbling and scrambling, through the thorny night-time underbrush of some German *schwarzwald*, a Jewish baby clamped to each of her tits, another brood of infants clinging to her back. Lilly clambers her way, struggling against the brambles that snag the gold embroidery of her **Balenciaga** lounging pajamas, the black velvet clutched by hordes of doomed cherubs she's racing to deliver from the ovens of some Nazi death camp. More innocent toddlers, lashed to each of Lillian's muscular thighs. Helpless Jewish, Gypsy and homosexual babies. Nazi gestapo bullets spit past her in the darkness, shredding the forest foliage, the smell of gunpowder and pine needles. The heady aroma of her **Chanel No. 5.** Bullets and hand grenades just whiz past Miss Hellman's perfectly coiffed **Hattie Carnegie** chignon, so close the ammunition shatters her **Cartier** chandelier earrings into rainbow explosions of priceless diamonds. Ruby and emerald shrapnel blasts into the flawless skin of her perfect, pale cheeks. . . . From this action sequence, we dissolve to:

Reveal: the interior of a stately **Sutton Place** mansion. It's some **Billie Burke** place decorated by **Billy Haines**, where formally dressed guests line a long table within a candlelit, wood-paneled dining room. Liveried footmen stand along the walls. Miss Hellman is seated near the head of this very large dinner party, actually describing the frantic escape scene we've just witnessed. In a slow panning shot, the engraved place cards denoting each guest read like a veritable **Who's Who**. Easily half of twentieth-century history sits at this table: **Prince Nicholas of Romania**, **Pablo Picasso**, **Cordell Hull** and **Josef von Sternberg**. The attendant celebrities seem to stretch from **Samuel Beckett** to **Gene Autry** to **Marjorie Main** to the faraway horizon.

Lillian stops speaking long enough to draw one long drag on her cigarette. Then to blow the smoke over **Pola Negri** and **Adolph Zukor** before she says, "It's at that heart-stopping moment I wished I'd just told **Franklin Delano Roosevelt**, 'No, thank you.'" Lilly taps cigarette ash onto her bread plate, shaking her head, saying, "No secret missions for this girl."

While the footmen pour wine and clear the sorbet dishes, Lillian's hands swim through the air, her cigarette trailing smoke, her fingernails clawing at invisible forest vines, climbing sheer rock cliff faces, her high heels blazing a muddy trail toward freedom, her strength never yielding under the burden of those tiny Jewish and homosexual urchins.

Every eye, fixed, from the head of the table to the foot, stares at Lilly. Every hand crosses two fingers beneath the damask napkin laid in every lap, while every guest mouths a silent prayer that Miss Hellman will swallow her **Chicken Prince Anatole Demidoff** without chewing, then suffocate, writhing and choking on the dining room carpet.

Almost every eye. The exceptions being one pair of violet eyes . . . one pair of brown eyes . . . and of course my own weary eyes.

The possibility of dying before **Lillian Hellman** has become the tangible fear of this entire generation. Dying and becoming merely fodder for Lilly's mouth. A person's entire life and reputation reduced to some **golem**, a **Frankenstein**'s monster Miss Hellman can reanimate and manipulate to do her bidding.

Beyond her first few words, Lillian's talk becomes one of those jungle sound tracks one hears looping in the background of every **Tarzan** film, just tropical birds and **Johnny Weissmuller** and howler monkeys repeating. *Bark, bark, screech* . . . **Emerald Cunard**. *Bark, growl, screech* . . . **Cecil Beaton**.

Lilly's drivel possibly constitutes some bizarre form of name-dropping **Tourette's syndrome**. Or perhaps the outcome of an orphaned press agent raised by wolves and taught to read aloud from **Walter Winchell**'s column.

Her compulsive prattle, a true pathology.

Cluck, oink, bark . . . **Jean Negulesco**.

Thus, Lilly spins the twenty-four-carat gold of people's actual lives into her own brassy straw.

Please promise you did *NOT* hear this from me.

Seated within range of those flying heroic elbows, my Miss Kathie stares out from the bank of cigarette smoke. An actress of **Katherine Kenton**'s stature. Her violet eyes, trained throughout her adult life to never make contact with anything except the lens of a motion picture camera. To never meet the eyes of a stranger, instead to always focus on someone's earlobe or lips. Despite such training, my Miss Kathie peers down the length of the table, her lashes fluttering. The slender fingers of one famous white hand toy with the auburn tresses of her wig. The jeweled fingers of Miss Kathie's opposite hand touch the six strands of pearls which contain the loose folds of her sagging neck skin.

In the next instant, while the footmen pass the finger bowls, Lillian twists in her chair, shouldering an invisible sniper's rifle and squeezing off rounds until the clip is empty. Still just dripping with Hebrew and Communist babies. Lugging her cargo of Semitic orphans. When the rifle is too searing hot to hold, Miss Hellman howls a wild war whoop and hurtles the steaming weapon at the pursuing storm troopers.

Snarl, bark, screech . . . **Peter Lorre.** *Oink, bark, squeal* . . . **Averill Harriman.**

It's a fate worse than death to spend eternity in harness, serving as Lilly Hellman's zombie, brought back to life at dinner parties. On radio talk programs. At this point, Miss Hellman is heaving yet another batch of invisible babies, rescued Gypsy babes, high, toward the chandelier, as if catapulting them over the snowcapped peak of the **Matterhorn** to the safety of **Switzerland.**

Grunt, howl, squeal . . . **Sarah Bernhardt.**

By now, **Lillian Hellman** wraps two fists around the invisible throat of **Adolf Hitler,** reenacting how she sneaked into his subterranean **Berlin** bunker, dressed as **Leni Riefenstahl,** her arms laden with black-market cartons of **Lucky Strike** and **Parliament** cigarettes, and then throttled the sleeping dictator in his bed.

Bray, bark, whinny . . . **Basil Rathbone.**

Lilly throws the terrified, make-believe Hitler into the center of tonight's dinner table, her teeth biting, her manicured fingernails scratching at his Nazi eyes. Lillian's fists clamped around the invisible windpipe, she begins pounding the invisible Führer's skull against the tablecloth, making the silverware and wineglasses jump and rattle.

Screech, meow, tweet . . . **Wallis Simpson.**

Howl, bray, squeak . . . **Diana Vreeland.**

A moment before Hitler's assassination, **George Cukor** looks up, his fingertips still dripping chilled water into his finger bowl, that smell of fresh-sliced lemons, and George says, "Please, Lillian." Poor George says, "Would you please *stuff* it."

Seated well below the salt, below the various professional hangers-on, the walking men, the drug dealers, the mesmerists, the exiled White Russians and poor **Lorenz Hart**, really at the very horizon of tonight's dinner table, a young man looks back. Seated on the farthest frontier of placement. His eyes the bright brown of July Fourth sunlight through a tall mug of root beer. Quite the American specimen. A classic face of such symmetrical proportions, the exactly balanced type of face one dreams of looking down to find smiling and eager between one's inner thighs.

Still, that's the trouble with only a single glance at any star on the horizon. As **Elsa Maxwell** would say, "One can never tell for certain if that dazzling, shiny object is rising or setting."

Lillian inhales the silence through her burning cigarette. Taps the gray ash onto her bread plate. In a blast of smoke, she says, "Did you hear?" She says, "It's a fact, but **Eleanor Roosevelt** chewed every hair off my bush. . . ."

Through all of this—the cigarette smoke and lies and the **Second World War**—the specimen's bright brown eyes, they're looking straight down the table, up the social ladder, gazing back, deep, into the famous, fluttering violet eyes of my employer.

ACT I, SCENE TWO

If you'll permit me to break the fourth wall, my name is **Hazie Coogan**.

My vocation is not that of a paid companion, nor am I a professional housekeeper. It is my role as an old woman to scrub the same pots and pans I scrubbed as a young one—I've made my peace with that fact—and while she has never once touched them, those pots and pans have always belonged to the majestic, the glorious film actress Miss **Katherine Kenton**.

It is my task to soft-boil her daily egg. I wax her linoleum kitchen floor. The endless job of dusting and polishing the not insignificant number of bibelots and gold-plated gimcracks awarded to Miss Katie, that job is mine as well. But am I Miss **Katherine Kenton**'s maid? No more so than the butcher plays handmaiden to the tender lamb.

My purpose is to impose order on Miss Kathie's chaos . . . to instill discipline in her legendary artistic caprice. I am the person **Lolly Parsons** once referred to as a "surrogate spine."

While I may vacuum the carpets of Miss Kathie's household and place the orders with the grocer, my true job title is not majordomo so much as mastermind. It might appear that Miss Kathie is my employer in the sense that she seems to provide me funds in exchange for my time and labor, and that she relaxes and blooms while I toil; but using that same logic, it could be argued that the farmer is employed by the pullet hen and the rutabaga.

The elegant **Katherine Kenton** is no more my master than the piano is master to **Ignace Jan Paderewski** . . . to paraphrase **Joseph L. Mankiewicz**, who paraphrased me, who first said and did most of the dazzling, clever things which, later, helped make others famous. In that sense you already know me. If you've seen **Linda Darnell** as a truck-stop waitress, sticking a pencil behind one ear in *Fallen Angel*, you've seen me. Darnell stole that bit from me. As does **Barbara Lawrence** when she brays her donkey laugh in *Oklahoma*. So many great actresses have filched my most effective mannerisms, and my spot-on delivery, that you've seen bits of me in performances by **Alice Faye** and **Margaret Dumont** and **Rise Stevens**. You'd recognize fragments of me—a raised eyebrow, a nervous hand twirling the cord of a telephone receiver—from countless old pictures.

The irony does not escape me that while **Eleanor Powell** lays claim to my fashion signature of wearing numerous small bows, I now boast the red knees of a charwoman and the swollen hands of a scullery maid. No less of an illustrious wag than **Darryl Zanuck** once dismissed me as looking like

Clifton Webb in a glen plaid skirt. **Mervyn LeRoy** spread the rumor that I am the secret love child of **Wally Beery** and his frequent costar **Marie Dressler**.

Currently, the regular duties of my position include defrosting Miss Kathie's electric icebox and ironing her bed linens, yet my position is not that of a laundress. My career is not as a cook. Nor is domestic servant my vocation. My life is far less steered by **Katherine Kenton** than her life is by me. Miss Kathie's daily demands and needs may determine my actions but only so much as the limits of a racing automobile will dictate those of the driver.

I am not merely a woman who works in a factory producing the ever-ravishing **Katherine Kenton**. I am the factory itself. With the words I write here I am not simply a camera operator or cinematographer; I am the lens itself—flattering, accentuating, distorting—recording how the world will recall my coquettish Miss Kathie.

Yet I am not just a sorceress. I am the source.

Miss Kathie exerts only a very small effort to be herself. The bulk of that manual labor is supplied by me in tandem with a phalanx of wig makers, plastic surgeons and dietitians. Since her earliest days under a studio contract it has been my livelihood to comb and dress her often blond, sometimes brunette, occasionally red hair. I coach the dulcet tones of her voice so as to make every utterance suggest a line of dialogue scripted for her by **Thornton Wilder**. Nothing of Miss Kathie is innate except for the almost supernatural violet coloring of her eyes. Hers is the throne, seated in the same icy pantheon as **Greta Garbo** and **Grace Kelly** and **Lana Turner**, but mine is the heavy lifting which keeps her on high.

And while the goal of every well-trained household servant is to seem invisible, that is also the goal of any accomplished puppeteer. Under my control, Miss Kathie's household seems to smoothly run itself, and she appears to run her own life.

My position is not that of a nurse, or a maid, or a secretary. Nor do I serve as a professional therapist or a chauffeur or bodyguard. While my job title is none of the preceding, I do perform all of those functions. Every evening, I pull the drapes. Walk the dog. Lock the doors. I disconnect the telephone, to keep the outside world in its correct place. However, more and more my job is to protect Miss Kathie from herself.

Cut direct to an interior, nighttime. We see the lavish boudoir belonging to **Katherine Kenton**, immediately following tonight's dinner party, with my Miss Kathie locked behind her en suite bathroom door. From offscreen, we hear the hiss and splash of a shower bath at full blast.

Despite popular speculation, Miss **Katherine Kenton** and I do not enjoy what **Walter Winchell** would call a "fingers-deep friendship." Nor do we indulge in behavior *Confidential* would cite to brand us as "baritone babes," or **Hedda Hopper** describes as "pink pucker sucking." The duties of my position include placing one **Nembutal** and one **Luminal** in the cloisonné saucer atop Miss Kathie's bedside table. In addition, filling an old-fashioned glass to overflowing with ice cubes and drop-by-drop pouring one shot of whiskey over the ice. Repeat with a second shot. Then fill the remainder of the glass with soda water.

The bedside table consists of nothing more than a stack of screenplays. A teetering pile sent by **Ruth Gordon** and **Garson Kanin**, asking my Miss Kathie to make a comeback. Begging, in fact. Here were speculative Broadway musicals based on actors dressed as dinosaurs or **Emma Goldman**.

Feature-length animated versions of *Macbeth* by **William Shakespeare** depicted with baby animals. Voice-over work. The pitch: **Bertolt Brecht** meets **Lerner and Loewe** crossed with **Eugene O'Neill**. The pages turn yellow and curl, stained with Scotch whiskey and cigarette smoke. The paper branded with the brown rings left by every cup of Miss Kathie's black coffee.

We repeat this ritual every evening, following whatever dinner party or opening my Miss Kathie has attended. On returning to her town house, I unfasten the eye hook at the top of her gown and release the zipper. Turn on the television. Change the channel. Change the television channel once more. Dump the contents of her evening bag onto the satin coverlet of her bed, Miss Kathie's **Helena Rubinstein** lipstick, keys, charge cards, replacing each item into her daytime bag. I place the shoe trees within her shoes. Pin her auburn wig to its **Styrofoam** head. Next, I light the vanilla-scented candles lined up along the mantel of her bedroom fireplace.

As my Miss Kathie conducts herself behind the en suite bathroom door, amid the rush and steam of her shower bath, her voice through the door drones: *bark, moo, meow* . . . **William Randolph Hearst**. *Snarl, squeal, tweet* . . . **Anita Loos**.

In the center of the satin bed sprawls her Pekingese, **Loverboy**, amid a field of wrinkled paper wrappers, the two cardboard halves of a heart-shaped candy box, the pleated pink brocade-and-silk roses stapled to the box cover, the ruched folds of lace frilling the box edges. The bed's billowing red satin coverlet, spread with this mess, the cupped candy papers, the sprawling Pekingese dog.

From out of Miss Kathie's evening bag spills her cigarette

lighter, a pack of **Pall Mall** cigarettes, her tiny pill box paved with rubies and tourmalines and rattling with **Tuinal** and **Dexamyl**. *Bark, cluck, squeak* . . . **Nembutal**.

Roar, whinny, oink . . . **Seconal**.

Meow, tweet, moo . . . **Demerol**.

Then, fluttering down, falls a white card. Settling on the bed, an engraved place card from this evening's dinner. Against the white card stock, in bold, black letters, the name **Webster Carlton Westward III**.

What **Hedda Hopper** would call this moment—a "Hollywood lifetime"—expires.

A freeze-frame. An insert-shot of the small, white card lying on the satin bed beside the inert dog.

On television, my Miss Kathie acts the part of Spain's **Queen Isabella I**, escaped from her royal duties in **the Alhambra** for a quickie vacation in **Miami Beach**, pretending to be a simple circus dancer in order to win the heart of **Christopher Columbus**, played by **Ramon Novarro**. The picture cuts to a cameo by **Lucille Ball**, on loan out from **Warner Bros.** and cast as Miss Kathie's rival, **Queen Elizabeth I**.

Here is all of Western history, rendered the bitch of **William Wyler**.

Behind the bathroom door, in the gush of hot water, my Miss Kathie says: *bark, bray, oink* . . . **J. Edgar Hoover**. My ears straining to hear her prattle.

Fringe dangles off the edge of the red satin coverlet, the bed canopy, the window valance. Everything upholstered in red velvet, cut velvet. Flocked wallpaper. The scarlet walls, padded and button tufted, crowded with **Louis XIV** mirrors. The lamps, dripping with faceted crystals, busy with sparkling thingamabobs. The fireplace, carved from pink onyx and rose quartz. The entire effect, insular and silent as sleeping tucked deep inside **Mae West's** vagina.

The four-poster bed, its trim and moldings lacquered red, polished until the wood looks wet. Lying there, the candy wrappers, the dog, the place card.

Webster Carlton Westward III, the American specimen with bright brown eyes. Root-beer eyes. The young man seated so far down the table at tonight's dinner. A telephone number, handwritten, a prefix in **Murray Hill**.

On the television, **Joan Crawford** enters the gates of **Madrid**, wearing some gauzy harem getup, both her hands carrying a wicker basket in front of her, the basket spilling over with potatoes and Cuban cigars, her bare limbs and face painted black to suggest she's a captured Mayan slave. The subtext being either Crawford's carrying syphilis or she's supposed to be a secret cannibal. Tainted spoils of the New World. A concubine. Perhaps she's an Aztec.

That slight lift of one naked shoulder, Crawford's shrug of disdain, here is another signature gesture stolen from me.

Above the mantel hangs a portrait of Miss Katherine painted by **Salvador Dalí**; it rises from a thicket of engraved invitations and the silver-framed photographs of men whom **Walter Winchell** would call "was-bands." Former husbands. The painting of my Miss Kathie, her eyebrows arch in surprise, but her heavy eyelashes droop, the eyelids almost closed with boredom. Her hands spread on either side of her face, her fingers fanning from her famous cheekbones to disappear into her movie star updo of auburn hair. Her mouth something between a laugh and a yawn. **Valium** and **Dexedrine**. Between **Lillian Gish** and **Tallulah Bankhead**. The portrait rises from the invitations and photographs, future parties and past marriages, the flickering candles and half-dead cigarettes stubbed out in crystal ashtrays threading white smoke upward in looping incense trails. This altar to my **Katherine Kenton**.

Me, forever guarding this shrine. Not so much a servant as a high priestess.

In what Winchell would call a "New York minute" I carry the place card to the fireplace. Dangle it within a candle flame until it catches fire. With one hand, I reach into the fireplace, deep into the open cavity of carved pink onyx and rose quartz, grasping in the dark until my fingers find the damper and wrench it open. Holding the white card, **Webster Carlton Westward III**, twisting him in the chimney draft, I watch a flame eat the name and telephone number. The scent of vanilla. The ash falls to the cold hearth.

On the television, **Preston Sturges** and **Harpo Marx** enter as **Tycho Brahe** and **Copernicus**. The first arguing that the earth goes around the sun, the latter insisting the world actually orbits **Rita Hayworth**. The picture is called *Armada of Love*, and **David O. Selznick** shot it on the **Universal** back lot the year when every other song on the radio was **Helen O'Connell** singing "**Bewitched, Bothered and Bewildered**," backed by the **Jimmy Dorsey** band.

The bathroom door swings open, Miss Kathie's voice saying: *bark, yip, cluck-cluck* . . . **Maxwell Anderson**. Her **Katherine Kenton** hair turbaned in a white bath towel. Her face layered with a mask of pulped avocado and royal jelly. Pulling the belt of her robe tight around her waist, my Miss Kathie looks at the lipstick dumped on her bed. The scattered cigarette lighter and keys and charge cards. The empty evening bag. Her gaze wafts to me standing before the fireplace, the tongues of candle flame licking below her

portrait, her lineup of "was-bands," the invitations, all those future obligations to enjoy herself, and—of course—the flowers.

Perched on the mantel, that altar, always enough flowers for a honeymoon suite or a funeral. Tonight features a tall arrangement of white spider chrysanthemums, white lilies and sprays of yellow orchids, bright and frilly as a cloud of butterflies.

With one hand, Miss Kathie sweeps aside the lipstick and keys, the cigarette pack, and she settles herself on the satin bed, amid the candy wrappers, saying, "Did you burn something just now?"

Katherine Kenton remains among the generation of women who feel that the most sincere form of flattery is the male erection. Nowadays, I tell her that erections are less likely a compliment than they are the result of some medical breakthrough. Transplanted monkey glands, or one of those new miracle pills.

As if human beings—men in particular—need yet another way to lie.

I ask, Did she misplace something?

Her violet eyes waft to my hands. Petting her Pekingese, **Loverboy**, dragging one hand through the dog's long fur, Miss Kathie says, "I do get so tired of buying my own flowers. . . ."

My hands, smeared black and filthy from the handle of the fireplace damper. Smudged with soot from the burned place card. I wipe them in the folds of my tweed skirt. I tell her I was merely disposing of some trash. Only incinerating a random piece of worthless trash.

On television, **Leo G. Carroll** kneels while **Betty Grable** crowns him **Emperor Napoleon Bonaparte. Pope Paul IV** is **Robert Young. Barbara Stanwyck** plays a gum-chewing **Joan of Arc.**

My Miss Kathie watches herself, seven divorces ago—what Winchell would call "Reno-vations"—and three face-lifts ago, as she grinds her lips against Novarro's lips. A specimen Winchell would call a "Wildeman." Like **Dorothy Parker's** husband, **Alan Campbell**, a man **Lillian Hellman** would call a "fairy shit." Petting her Pekingese with long licks of her hand, Miss Kathie says, "His saliva tasted like the wet dicks of ten thousand lonely truck drivers."

Next to her bed, the night table built from a thousand hopeful dreams, those balanced screenplays, it supports two barbiturates and a double whiskey. Miss Kathie's hand stops petting and scratching the dog's muzzle; there the fur looks dark and matted. She pulls back her arm, and the towel slips from her head, her hair tumbling out, limp and gray, pink scalp showing between the roots. The green mask of her avocado face cracking with her surprise.

Miss Kathie looks at her hand, and the fingers and palm are smeared and dripping with dark red.

Katherine Kenton lived as a **Houdini**. An escape artist. It didn't matter . . . marriages, funny farms, airtight **Pandro Berman** studio contracts . . . My Miss Kathie trapped herself because it felt such a triumph to slip the noose at the eleventh hour. To foil the legal boilerplate binding her to bad touring projects with **Red Skelton**. The approach of **Hurricane Hazel**. Or the third trimester of a pregnancy by **Huey Long**. Always one clock tick before it was too late, my Miss Kathie would take flight.

Here, let's make a slow dissolve to flashback. To the year when every other song on the radio was **Patti Page** singing "(**How Much Is**) **That Doggy in the Window?**" The mise-en-scène shows the daytime interior of a basement kitchen in the elegant town house of **Katherine Kenton**; arranged along the upstage wall: an electric stove, an icebox, a door to the alleyway, a dusty window in said door.

In the foreground, I sit on a white-painted kitchen chair with my feet propped on a similar table, my legs crossed at the ankle, my hands holding a ream of paper. A note flutters, held by paper clip to the title page. In slanted handwriting the note reads: *I demand you savor this while it still reeks of my sweat and loins.* Signed, **Lillian Hellman.**

Nothing is ever so much signed by Lilly as it is autographed.

On page one of the screenplay, **Robert Oppenheimer** puzzles over the best method for accelerating particle diffusion until Lillian stubs out a **Lucky Strike** cigarette, tosses back a shot of **Dewar's whiskey**, and elbows Oppenheimer away from the rambling equation chalked the length of a vast blackboard. Using spit and her **Max Factor** eyebrow pencil, Lilly alters the speed of enriched uranium fission while **Albert Einstein** looks on. Slapping himself on the forehead with the palm of one hand, Einstein says, "Lilly, *meine liebchen, du bist eine genious!*"

At the window of the kitchen door, something outside taps. A bird in the alley, pecking. The sharp point of something tap, tap, taps at the glass. In the dawn sunlight, the shadow of something hovers just outside the dusty window, the shining point pecking, knocking tiny divots in the exterior surface of the glass. Some lost bird, starving in the cold. Digging, chipping tiny pits.

On the page, Lillian twists a copy of the *New Masses*, rolling it to fashion a tight baton which she swats across the face of **Christian Dior. Harry Truman** has herded together the world's top fashion mavens to brand the signature look of his ultimate weapon. **Coco Chanel** demands sequins. **Sister Parish** sketches the bomb screaming down from the Japanese sky trailing long bugle beads. **Elsa Schiaparelli** holds out for a quilted sateen slipcover. **Cristobal Balenciaga**, shoulder pads. **Mainbocher**, tweed. **Dior** scatters the conference room with swatches of plaid.

Brandishing her rolled billy club, Lilly says, "What happens if the zipper gets stuck?"

"Lilly, darling," says **Dior**, "it's a fucking atom bomb!"

At the kitchen window, the sharp beak drags itself against the outside of the glass, tracing a long curve, scratching the glass with an impossible, high-pitched shriek. An instant migraine headache, the point traces a second curve. The two curves combine to form a heart, etched into the window, and the dragging point plows an arrow through the heart.

On paper, **Adrian** sees the entirety of the atom bomb encrusted with a thick layer of rhinestones, flashing a dazzling Allied victory. **Edith Head** pounds her small fist on the conference table at the **Waldorf=Astoria** and proclaims that something hand-crocheted must rain fiery death on **Hirohito**, or she'll pull out of the **Manhattan Project**. **Hubert de Givenchy** pounds on **Pierre Balmain**.

I stand and cross to the alley door. There we discover my Miss Kathie standing in the alley, bundled in a fur coat, both arms folded across her chest, hugging herself in the cold dawn.

I ask, Isn't she home a few months early?

And Miss Kathie says, "I found something so much better than sobriety. . . ." She waves the back of her left hand, the ring finger flashing with a **Harry Winston** diamond solitaire, and she says, "I found **Paco Esposito!**"

The diamond, the tool she used to cut her heart so deep into the glass. The heart and **Cupid**'s arrow etched in the alley window. Yet another engagement ring she's bought herself.

Behind her stands a young man hung like a Christmas tree with various pieces of luggage: purses, garment bags, suitcases and satchels. All of it **Louis Vuitton**. He wears blue denim trousers, the knees stained black with motor oil. The sleeves of his blue chambray shirt rolled high to reveal tattooed arms. His name, Paco, embroidered on one side of his chest. His cologne, the stench of high-test gasoline.

Miss Kathie's violet eyes twitch side to side across my face, up and down, the way they'd vacuum up last-minute rewrites in dialogue.

The sole reason for **Katherine Kenton**'s admitting herself to any hospital was because she so enjoyed the escape. Between making pictures, she craved the drama of overcoming locked doors, barred windows, sedatives and straitjackets. Stepping indoors from the cold alley, her breath steaming, my Miss Kathie wears cardboard slippers. Not **Madeleine Vionnet**. She wears a tissue-paper gown under her silver fox coat. Not **Vera Maxwell**. Miss Kathie's cheeks scrubbed pink from the sun. The wind has tossed her auburn hair into heavy waves. Her blue fingers grip the handles of a shopping bag she lifts to set atop the kitchen table.

In the screenplay's third act, Hellman pilots the controls of the *Enola Gay* as it skims the tops of Japanese pine trees and giant pandas and **Mount Fuji**, en route to **Hiroshima**. In a fantasy sequence, we cut to Hellman wielding a machete to castrate a screaming **Jack Warner**. She skins alive a bellowing, bleeding **Louis B. Mayer**. Her grip tightens around the lever which opens the bomb bay doors. Her deadly cargo shimmers pristine as a bride, covered with seed pearls and fluttering white lace.

In her own kitchen, my Miss Kathie sinks both hands into the shopping bag and lifts out a hairy chunk of her fur coat. The ragged pile of hair seems to tremble as she places it atop the Hellman screenplay. Two black button eyes blink open. On the table, the damp, hairy wad shrinks, then explodes in a *hah-choo* sneeze. Between the two button eyes, the fur parts to reveal a double row of needle teeth. A panting sliver of pink tongue. A puppy.

Around the new diamond ring, her movie star hands appear nicked and scabbed with dried red, smudged with old blood. Spreading her fingers to show me the backs of both hands, Miss Kathie says, "This hospital had barbed wire."

Her barbed wire scars as gruesome as any wounds Lillian shows off from the **Abraham Lincoln** brigade. Not as bad as **Ava Gardner**'s scars from bullfighting with **Ernest Hemingway**. Or **Gore Vidal**'s scars from **Truman Capote**.

"I picked up a stray," says Miss Kathie.

I ask, Which one? The dog or the man?

"It's a Pekingese," says Miss Kathie. "I've christened him **Loverboy**."

The most recent of the "was-bands," Paco arrives after the senator who arrived after the faggot chorus boy who arrived after the steel-smelting tycoon who arrived after the failed actor who arrived after the sleazy freelance photographer who arrived after the high school sweetheart. These, all of the stray dogs whose photographs line the mantel in her lavish upstairs boudoir.

A rogues' gallery of what **Walter Winchell** would call "happily-never-afters."

Each romance, the type of self-destructive gesture **Hedda Hopper** would call "marry-kiri." Instead of plunging a sword into one's stomach, you repeatedly throw yourself on the most inappropriate erect penis.

The men Miss Katherine marries, they're less husbands

than they are costars. Souvenirs. Each one merely a witness to attest to her latest daring adventure, so much like **Raymond Massey** or **Fredric March**, any leading man she might fight beside in the **Hundred Years War**. Playing **Amelia Earhart** stowed away with champagne and **beluga caviar** in the romantic cockpit of **Charles Lindbergh** during his long flight over the Atlantic. **Cleopatra** kidnapped during the Crusades and wed to **King Henry VIII**.

Each wedding picture was less of a memento than a scar. Proof of some horror movie scenario **Katherine Kenton** has survived.

Miss Kathie places the puppy on the Hellman screenplay, smack-dab on the scene where Lilly Hellman and **John Wayne** raise the American flag over **Iwo Jima**. Dipping one scabbed hand into the pocket of her silver fox coat, Miss Kathie extracts a tablet of bound papers, each page printed with the letterhead *White Mountain Hospital and Residential Treatment Facility*.

A purloined pad of prescription blanks.

Miss Kathie wets the point of an **Estée Lauder** eyebrow pencil, touching it against the pink tip of her tongue. Writing a few words under the letterhead, she stops, looks up and says, "How many Ss in *Darvocet*?"

The young man holding her baggage says, "How soon do we get to **Hollywood**?"

Los Angeles, the city **Louella Parsons** would call the approximately three hundred square miles and twelve million people centered around **Irene Mayer Selznick**.

In that same beat, we cut to a close-up of **Loverboy**, as the tiny Pekingese drops its own hot, stinking A-bomb all over **General Douglas MacArthur**.

ACT I, SCENE FOUR

The career of a movie star consists of helping everyone else forget their troubles. Using charm and beauty and good cheer to make life look easy. "The problem is," **Gloria Swanson** once said, "if you never weep in public . . . well, the public assumes you never weep."

Act one, scene four opens with **Katherine Kenton** cradling an urn in her arms. The setting: the dimly lit interior of the Kenton crypt, deep underground, below the stony pile of **St. Patrick's Cathedral**, dressed with cobwebs. We see the ornate bronze door unlocked and swung open to welcome mourners. A stone shelf at the rear of the crypt, in deep shadow, holds various urns crafted from a variety of polished metals, bronze, copper, nickel, one engraved, *Casanova*, another engraved, *Darling*, another, *Romeo*.

My Miss Kathie hugs the urn she's holding, lifting it to

meet her lips. She plants a puckered lipstick kiss on the engraved name *Loverboy*, then places this new urn on the dusty shelf among the others.

Kay Francis hasn't arrived. **Humphrey Bogart** didn't send his regards. Neither did **Deanna Durbin** or **Mildred Coles**. Also missing are **George Bancroft** and **Bonita Granville** and **Frank Morgan**. None of them sent flowers.

The engraved names *Sweetie Pie* and *Honey Bun* and *Oliver "Red" Drake, Esq.*, what **Hedda Hopper** would call "dust buddies." Her beagle, her Chihuahua, her fourth husband—the majority stockholder and chairman of the board for **International Steel Manufacturing**. Scattered amongst the other urns, engraved: *Pookie*, and *Fantasy Man*, and *Lothario*, the ashen remains of her toy poodle and miniature pinscher, there also sits an orange plastic prescription bottle of **Valium**, tethered to the stone shelf by a net of spiderwebs. Mold and dust mottle the label on a bottle of **Napoleon brandy**. A pharmacy prescription bottle of **Luminal**.

What **Louella Parsons** would call "moping mechanisms."

My Miss Kathie leans forward to blow the dust from a pill bottle. She lifts the bottle and wrestles the tricky child-guard cap, soiling her black gloves, pressing the cap as she twists, the pills inside rattling. Echoing loud as machine-gun fire in the cold stone room. My Miss Kathie shakes a few pills into one gloved palm. With the opposite hand, she lifts her black veil. She tosses the pills into her mouth and reaches for the crusted bottle of brandy.

Among the urns, a silver picture frame lies facedown on the shelf. Next to it, a tarnished tube of **Helena Rubinstein** lipstick. A slow panning shot reveals an atomizer of **Mitsouko**, the crystal bottle clouded and smudged with fingerprints. A dusty box spouts yellowed **Kleenex** tissues.

In the dim light, we see a bottle of vintage 1851 **Château Lafite**. A magnum of **Huet calvados**, circa 1865, and **Croizet cognac** bottled in 1906. **Campbell Bowden & Taylor** port, vintage 1825.

Stacked against the stone walls are cases of **Dom Pérignon** and **Moët & Chandon** and **Bollinger** champagne in bottles of every size . . . **Jeroboam** bottles, named for the biblical king, son of **Nebat** and **Zeruah**, which hold as much as four typical wine bottles. Here are **Nebuchadnezzar** bottles, twenty times the size of a typical bottle, named for a king of **Babylon**. Among those tower **Melchior** bottles, which hold the equivalent of twenty-four bottles of champagne, named for one of the **Three Wise Men** who greeted the birth of **Jesus Christ**. As many bottles stand empty as still corked. Empty wineglasses litter the cold shadows, long ago abandoned, smudged by the lips of **Conrad Nagel**, **Alan Hale**, **Cheeta the chimp** and **Bill Demarest**.

Miss Kathie's mourning veil falls back, covering her face, and she drinks through the black netting, holding each bottle to her lips and swigging, leaving a new layer of lipstick caked around each new bottle's glistening neck. Each bottle's mouth as red as her own.

Sydney Greenstreet, another no-show at today's funeral. **Greta Garbo** did not send her sympathies.

What **Walter Winchell** calls "stiff standing up."

Here we are, just Miss Katherine and myself, yet again.

Brushing aside the black rice of mouse feces—in this strange negative image of a wedding—my Miss Kathie lifts the silver picture frame and props it to stand on the shelf, leaning the frame against the tomb's wall. Instead of a picture, the frame surrounds a mirror. Within the mirror, within the reflection of the stone walls, the cobwebs, poses Miss Kathie wearing her black hat and veil. She pinches the fingertips of one glove, pulling the glove free of her left hand. Twisting the diamond solitaire off her ring finger, she hands the six-carat, marquise-cut **Harry Winston** to me. Miss Kathie says, "I guess we ought to record the moment."

The mirror, old scratches scar and etch its surface. The glass marred by a wide array of old scores.

I tell her, Hit your mark, please.

"Are you absolutely certain you phoned **Cary Grant**?" says Miss Kathie as she steps backward and stands on a faded X, long ago marked in lipstick on the stone floor. At that precise point her movie-star face aligns perfectly with the scratches on the mirror. At that perfect angle and distance, those old scores become the wrinkles she had three, four, five dogs ago, the bags and sumps her face fell into before each was repaired with a new face-lift or an injection of sheep embryo serum. Some radical procedure administered in a secret Swiss clinic. The expensive creams and salves, the operations to pull and tighten. On the mirror linger the pits and liver spots she has erased every few months, etched there—the record of how she ought to look. Again, she lifts her veil, and her reflected cheeks and chin align with the ancient record of sags and moles and stray hairs my Miss Kathie has rightfully earned.

The war wounds left by **Paco Esposito** and **Romeo**, every stray dog and "was-band."

Miss Kathie makes the face she makes when she's not making a face, her features, her famous mouth and eyes becoming a **Theda Bara** negligee draped over a padded hanger in the back of the **Monogram Pictures** wardrobe department, wrapped in plastic in the dark. Her muscles slack and relaxed. The audience forgotten.

And wielding the diamond, I get to work, drawing. I trace any new wrinkles, adding any new liver spots to this long-term record. Creating something more cumulative than any photograph, I document Miss Kathie's misery before the plastic surgeons can once more wipe the slate clean. Dragging the diamond, digging into the glass, I etch her gray hairs. Updating the topography of this, her secret face. Cutting the latest worry lines across her forehead. I gouge the new crow's-feet around her eyes, eclipsing the false smile of her public image, the diamond defacing Miss Kathie. Me mutilating her.

After a lifetime of such abuse the mirror bows, curved, so sectioned, so cut and etched so deep, that any new pressure could collapse the glass into a shattered, jagged pile of fragments. Another duty of my job is to never press too hard. My position included mopping up Paco's piss from around the commode, then taking the dog to a veterinarian for gelding. Every day, I was compelled to tear a page from some history book—the saga of **Hiawatha**, written by **Arthur Miller** as a screenplay for **Deborah Kerr**, or the **Robert Fulton** story, as a vehicle for **Danny Kaye**—to pick up yet another steaming handful of feces.

I drag the diamond in straight lines to mimic the tears running down Miss Kathie's face.

The diamond shrieks against the glass. The sound of an instant migraine headache.

The mirror of **Dorian Gray**.

Then footsteps echo from offscreen. The heartbeat of a man's leather shoes approach from down the corridor, each step louder against the stone. **Van Heflin** or perhaps **Laurence Olivier**. **Randolph Scott** or maybe **Sid Luft**.

In the silence between one footfall and the next, between heartbeats, I place the mirror facedown on the shelf. I return the diamond ring to my Miss Kathie.

A man's silhouette fills the doorway to the crypt, tall and slender, his shoulders straight, outlined against the light of the corridor.

Miss Kathie turns, one hand already reaching for the tarnished tube of lipstick. She peers at the man, saying, "Could that be you, **Groucho**?"

A bouquet of flowers emerges out of the gloom, the man's hands offering them. Pink **Nancy Reagan** roses and yellow lilies, a smell bright as sunlight. The man's voice says, "I'm so sorry about your loss. . . ." The smooth knuckles and clear skin of a young man's hands, the fingernails shining and polished.

What **Hedda Hopper** calls a "funeral flirtation." **Louella Parsons** a "graveside groom." **Walter Winchell** a "casket crasher."

Webster Carlton Westward III steps forward. The young man from the dinner party. The name and phone number on the burned place card.

Those eyes bright brown as summer root beer.

I shake my head, Don't. Don't repeat this torture. Don't trust another one.

But already my Miss Kathie wipes a fresh coat of red around her mouth. Then tosses the old lipstick to rattle among the tarnished urns. Among the empty wine bottles that people call "dead soldiers." My Miss Kathie lowers the black mesh of her veil and reaches one gloved hand toward something coated with dust, something abandoned and long forgotten among her dead loves. She lifts this ancient item, her red lips whispering, "*Guten essen.*" Adding, "That's French for 'never say never.'" Her violet eyes milky and vague with the drugs and brandy, Miss Kathie turns to accept the flowers, in the same gesture slipping the dusty item—her diaphragm—deep into the sagging slit of her old mink coat pocket.

Clare Boothe Luce once said the following about Katherine Kenton—"When she's in love, nothing can make her sad; however when she's not in love, nothing can make her happy."

We're playing this next scene in the bathroom adjacent to Miss Kathie's boudoir. As it opens, we discover my Miss Kathie seated at her dressing table, facing three mirrors angled to show her right profile, her left profile, and her full face. The bouquet of pink Nancy Reagan roses and yellow lilies delivered by Webster Carlton Westward III occupy a vase, those few flowers reflected and reflected until they could be a florist shop. An entire garden. This single bouquet, multiplied. Made infinite. Not left at the crypt to rot.

Dangling from the bouquet, a parchment card reads: *Our love is only wasted when we fail to share it with another. Please allow the world to share its limitless love with you.* Some gibberish plagiarized from John Milton or Mohandas Gandhi.

Reflected in the mirrors, my Miss Kathie pinches the slack skin that hangs below her chin. Pinching and pulling the skin, she says, "No more whiskey. And no more of those damned chocolates."

Chocolate poisoning, it fits all the earmarks. Shame on Miss Kathie for neglecting an entire box on her bed, where **Loverboy** would be bound to sniff them out. The caffeine contained in even a single bonbon more than sufficient to bring about a heart attack in a dog of that size.

The parchment card, signed, *Webb*. The Westward boy, what **Cholly Knickerbocker** would term an "opportunistic affection." Next to the roses on the polished top of her dressing table rests the rubber bump of Miss Kathie's diaphragm, pink rubber flocked with dust.

Peeling off her false eyelashes, Miss Kathie looks at me standing behind her, both of us reflected in the mirror, multiplied into a mob, the whole world peopled by just us two, and she says, "Are you certain that no one else sent their condolences?"

I shake my head, No. No one.

Miss Kathie peels off her auburn wig, handing it to me. She says, "Not even the senator?"

The "was-band" before Paco. **Senator Phelps Russell Warner**. Again, I shake my head, No. Not **Terrence Terry**, the faggot dancer. Not **Paco Esposito**, who currently plays a hot-tempered, flamenco-dancing Latin brain surgeon on some new radio program called *Guiding Light*. None of the was-bands have sent a word of condolence.

Pawing the makeup from her face with cotton balls and cold cream, Miss Kathie snaps the elastic wig cap off the crown of her head. Her movie-star hands claw the long strands of gray hair loose. She twists her head side to side, fast, so the hair fans out, hanging to the pink, padded shoulders of her satin dressing gown. Fingering a few wispy gray strands, Miss Kathie says, "Do you think my hair will hold dye again?"

The first symptom of what **Walter Winchell** calls "infant-uation" is when Miss Kathie colors her hair the bright orange of a tabby cat.

"Optimism," says **H. L. Mencken**, "is the first symptom that any disease is fatal."

Miss Kathie cups a hand beneath each of her breasts, lifting them until the cleavage swells at her throat. Watching herself in the angled mirrors, she says, "Why can't that brilliant **Dr. Josef Mengele** in **Munich** do something about my old-lady *hands*?"

At best, this young Westward specimen is what **Lolly Parsons** calls a "boy-ographer." One of those smiling, dancing young gadabouts who insinuate themselves in the private lives of lonely, fading motion-picture stars. Professional listeners, these meticulously well-groomed walking men, they listen to confidences, indulge strong egos and weakening minds, forever cherry-picking the best anecdotes and quotes, with a manuscript always ready for publication upon the instant of the movie star's demise. So many cozy evenings beside the fire, sipping brandy, those nights will pay off with scandalous confessions and declarations. Mr. Bright Brown Eyes, without a doubt, he's one of those seducers ready to betray every secret, every wart and flatulence of Miss Kathie's private life.

This Webster specimen is obviously a would-be author, looking to write the type of intimate tell-all that Winchell calls an unauthorized "bile-ography." The literary equivalent of a <u>magpie</u>, stealing the brightest and darkest moments from every celebrity he'll meet.

My Miss Kathie scoops a finger through a jar of **Vaseline**, then rubs a fat lump of the slime, smearing it across her top and bottom teeth, pushing her finger deep to coat her molars. She smiles her greasy smile and says, "Do you have a spoon?"

In the kitchen, I tell her. We haven't kept a spoon in her bathroom since the year when every other song on the radio was **Christine, Dorothy** and **Phyllis McGuire** singing "**Don't Take Your Love from Me**."

Miss Kathie's goal: to reduce until she becomes what **Lolly Parsons** calls nothing but "tan and bones." What **Hedda Hopper** calls a "lipstick skeleton." A "beautifully coiffed skull" as **Elsa Maxwell** calls **Katharine Hepburn**.

The moment of Miss Kathie's exit in search of said spoon, my fingers pry open a box of bath salts and pinch up the coarse grains. These I sprinkle between the roses, swirling the vase to dissolve the salts into the water. My fingers pluck the card from the bouquet of roses and lilies. Folding the parchment, I tear it once, twice. Folding and tearing until the sentences become only words. The words become only letters of the alphabet, which I sprinkle into the toilet bowl. As I flush the lever, the water rises in the bowl, the torn parchment spinning as the water deepens. From deep within itself, the commode regurgitates a hidden mess of paper trapped down within the toilet's throat. Bobbing to the surface, bits of waterlogged paper, greeting cards, the tissue paper of telegrams. It all backs up within the clogged bowl.

Within the rim of the toilet swirls a tide of affection and concern, signed by **Edna Ferber, Artie Shaw, Bess Truman**.

The handwritten notes and cards, the telegrams reading, *If there's anything I can do . . .* and, *Please don't hesitate to call.* The torn scraps of these sentiments spin higher and higher toward the brim of disaster, preparing to overflow, to run over the lip of the white bowl and flood the pink marble floor. These affectionate words . . . I've torn them into bits, and then torn those into smaller bits, scraps. All of my covert work is about to be exposed. These, all of the condolences I've destroyed during the past few days.

From the downstairs powder room, echoing up through the silence of the town house, the sounds of Miss Kathie's gorge rises with beef **Stroganoff** and **Queen Charlotte** pears and veal **Prince Orloff**, heaving up from the depths of Miss Kathie, triggered by the tip of a silver spoon touching the back of her tongue, her gag reflex rejecting it all.

"Fuck 'em," Miss Kathie says between splashes, her movie-star voice hoarse with bile and stomach acid. "They don't care," she says, purging herself in great thunderous blasts.

The infamous advice **Busby Berkeley** gave to **Judy Garland**, "If you're still having bowel movements, you're eating too much."

Upstairs, the shredded affections rise, about to spill out onto the bathroom floor. Spiraling upward toward disaster. At the last possible moment I drop to my knees on the pink marble tile. I plunge my hand into the churning mess, the cold water lapping around my elbow, then swirling about my shoulder as I burrow my hand deep into the toilet's throat, clearing aside wet paper. Clawing, scratching a tunnel through the sodden, matted layer of endearments. The soft mass of sentiments I can't see.

Downstairs, Miss Kathie heaves out great mouthfuls of gâteau **Pierre Rothschild**. Bombe de **Louise Grimaldi**. **Aunt**

Jemima syrup. **Lady Baltimore** cake. The wet, bubbling shouts of undigested **Jimmy Dean** sausage.

The plumbing of this old town house shudders, the pipes banging and thudding to contain and channel this new burden of macerated secrets and gourmet vomit.

A "Hollywood lifetime" later, the water in the toilet bowl begins to recede.

The shredded scraps of love and caring, the kind regards sink from sight. Freshwater chases the final words of comfort into the sewers. Those lacy, embossed, engraved and perfumed fragments, the toilet gulps them down. The water swallows every last word of sympathy from **Jeanne Crain**, the florid handwriting of **Her Royal Highness Princess Margaret**, from **John Gilbert, Linus Pauling** and **Christiaan Barnard**. In her bathroom, the purge of names and devotion signed, **Brooks Atkinson, George Arliss** and **Jill Esmond**, the spinning flood disappearing, disappearing, the water level drops until all the names and notes are sucked down. Drowned.

Echoing from the downstairs powder room comes the hawk and spit sound of my Miss Kathie clearing the bile taste from her mouth. Her cough and belch. A final flush of the downstairs commode, followed by the rushing spray noise of aerosol room deodorant.

A "New York second" goes by, and I stand. One step to the sink, and I calmly begin to scrub my dripping hands, careful to pick and scrape the words *sorrow* and *tragedy* from where they're lodged beneath each fingernail. Already, the lovely bouquet of pink roses and yellow lilies poisoned with salt water, the petals begin to wither and brown.

ACT I, SCENE SIX

The next sequence depicts a montage of flowers arriving at the town house. Deliverymen wearing jaunty, brimmed caps and polished shoes arrive to ring the front doorbell. Each man carries a long box of roses tied with a floppy velvet ribbon, tucked under one arm. Or a cellophane spill brimming full of roses cradled the way one would carry an infant. Each deliveryman's opposite hand extends, ready to offer a clipboard and a pen, a receipt needing a signature. Billowing masses of white lilac. Delivery after delivery arrives. The doorbell ringing to announce yellow gladiolas and scarlet birds-of-paradise. Trembling pink branches of dogwood in full bloom. The chilled flesh of hothouse orchids. Camellias. Each new florist always stretches his neck to see past me, craning his head to see into the foyer for a glimpse of the famous **Katherine Kenton**.

One frame too late, Miss Kathie's voice calls from offscreen, "Who is it?" The moment after the deliveryman is gone.

Me, always shouting in response, It's the Fuller Brush man. A Jehovah's Witness. A Girl Scout, selling cookies. The same *ding-dong* of the doorbell cueing the cut to another bouquet of honeysuckle or towering pink spears of flowering ginger.

Me, shouting up the stairs to Miss Kathie, asking if she expects a gentleman caller.

In response, Miss Kathie shouting, "No." Shouting, less loudly, "No one in particular."

In the foyer and dining room and kitchen, the air swims with the scent of phantom flowers, shimmering with sweet, heavy mock orange. An invisible garden. The creamy perfume of absent gardenias. Hanging in the air is the tang of eucalyptus I carry directly to the back door. The trash cans in the alley overflow with crimson bougainvillea and sprays of sweet-smelling daphne.

Every card signed, *Webster Carlton Westward III.*

From an insert shot of one gift card, we cut to a close-up of another card, and another. A series of card after gift card. Then a close-up of yet another paper envelope with *To Miss Katherine* handwritten on one side. The shot pulls back to reveal me holding this last sealed envelope in the steam jetting from a kettle boiling atop the stove. The kitchen setting appears much the same as it did a dog's lifetime ago, when my Miss Kathie scratched her heart into the window. One new detail, a portable television, sits atop the icebox, flashing the room with scenes from a hospital, the operating room in a surgical suite where an actor's rubber-gloved hand grasps a surgical mask and pulls it from his own face, revealing the previous "was-band," **Paco Esposito**. The seventh and most recent Mr. **Katherine Kenton**. His hair now grows gray at his temples. His upper lip fringed with a pepper-and-salt mustache.

The teakettle hisses on the stove, centered above the blue spider of a gas flame. Steam rises from the spout, curling the corners of the white envelope I hold. The paper darkens with damp until the glued flap peels along one edge. Picking with a thumbnail, I lift the flap. Pinching with two fingers, I slide out the letter.

On television, Paco leans over the operating table, dragging a scalpel through the inert body of a patient played by **Stephen Boyd**. **Hope Lange** plays the assisting physician. **Suzy Parker** the anesthesiologist. Fixing his gaze on the attending nurse, **Natalie Wood**, Paco says, "I've never seen anything this bad. This brain has got to come out!"

The next channel over, a battalion of dancers dash around a soundstage, fighting the **Battle of Antietam** in some **Frank Powell** production directed by **D. W. Griffith** of a musical version of the **Civil War**. The lead for the **Confederate Army**, leaping and pirouetting, is featured dancer **Terrence Terry**. A heartbreakingly young **Joan Leslie** plays **Tallulah Bankhead**. **H. B. Warner** plays **Jefferson Davis**. Music scored by **Max Steiner**.

From the alley outside the kitchen door, a man's voice says, "Knock, knock." The windows, fogged with the steam. The kitchen air feels humid and warm as the sauna of the **Garden of Allah** apartments. My hair hangs lank and plastered to my wet forehead, flat as a **Louise Brooks** spit curl.

The shadow of a head falls against the outside of the window, the pane where my Miss Kathie cut the shape of her heart. From behind the fogged glass, the voice says, "Kath-

erine?" His knuckles knocking the glass, a man says, "This is an emergency."

Unfolded, the letter reads: *My Most Dear Katherine, True love is NOT out of your reach.* I flatten the letter to the damp window glass, where it sticks, held secure as wallpaper, pasted there by the condensed steam. The sunlight streaming in from the alleyway, the light leaves the paper translucent, glowing white with the handwritten words hung framed by the heart etched in the glass. The letter still pasted to the window, I flip the dead bolt, slip the chain, turn the knob and open the door.

In the alleyway, a man stands holding a paper tablet fluttering with pages. Each page scribbled with names and arrows, what looks like the diagram for plays in a football game. Among the names one can read **Eve Arden . . . Marlene Dietrich . . . Sidney Blackmer . . .** In his opposite hand, the man holds a white paper sack. Next to him, the trash cans spill their roses and gardenias onto the paving stones. The gladiolas and orchids tumble out to lie in the fetid puddles of mud and rainwater which run down the center of the alley. The reek of honeysuckle and spoiled meat. Pale mock orange mingles with pink camellias and bloodred peonies.

"Hurry, quick, where's Lady Katherine?" the man says, holding the tablet, shaking it so the pages flap. On some, the names radiate in every direction from a large rectangle which fills the center of the page. The names alternating gender: **Lena Horne** then **William Wellman** then **Esther Williams**. The man says, "I'm expecting twenty-four guests for dinner, and I have a placement emergency. . . ."

The diagrams are seating charts. The rectangles are the dinner table. The names the guest list. "As added incentive," the man says, "tell Her Majesty that I've brought her favorite candy . . . **Jordan almonds**."

Her Majesty won't eat a bite, I tell him.

This man, this same face smiles out from the frontline skirmishes on television, amid the **Battle of Gettysburg**—this is **Terrence Terry**, formerly Mr. Katherine Kenton, former dancer under contract at **Lasky Studios**, former paramour to **Montgomery Clift**, former catamite to **James Whale** and **Don Ameche**, former cosodomite to **William Haines**, former sexual invert, the fifth "was-band," in crisis about whom to seat next to **Celeste Holm** at a dinner he's hosting tonight.

"This is an entertainment emergency," the Terrence specimen says, "I need Katherine to tell me: Does **Jack Buchanan** hate **Dame May Whitty?**"

I say that he should've gone to prison for wedding Miss Kathie. That it's illegal for homosexuals to get married.

"Only to each other," he says, stepping into the kitchen.

I close the alley door, lock the knob, slip the chain, flip the dead bolt.

Whatever the case, I say, a marriage isn't something one undertakes simply to pad one's résumé. Saying this, I'm retrieving a sheet of blank stationery from the kitchen table, then positioning this sheet on the damp window so that it aligns with the love letter already pasted to the glass.

"Her Majesty doesn't have to come dine with us," this **Terrence Terry** says. "Just tell me who to stick next to **Jane Wyman**."

Using a pen, blue ink, I begin to trace the writing of the original letter as it glows through this new, blank sheet.

"Lady Katherine can tell me if **John Agar** is right- or left-handed," says this Terrence specimen. "She knows if **Rin Tin Tin** is male or female."

Lecturing, still tracing the old letter onto the new paper, I suggest he begin with a fresh page. An empty dinner table. Seat **Desi Arnaz** to the left of **Hazel Court**. Put **Rosemary Clooney** across from **Lex Barker**. **Fatty Arbuckle** always spits as he speaks, so place him opposite **Billie Dove**, who's too blind to notice. Using my own pen, I elbow into Terry's work, drawing arrows from **Jean Harlow** to **Lon Chaney Sr.** to **Douglas Fairbanks Jr.** Like **Knute Rockne** sketching football plays, I circle **Gilda Gray** and **Hattie McDaniel**, and I cross out **June Haver**.

"If she's starving herself," says **Terrence Terry**, watching me work, "she must be falling in love again." Standing there, he unrolls the top of the white paper bag. Reaching into it, Terry lifts out a handful of almonds, pastel shades of pink and green and blue. He slips one into his mouth, chews.

Not only starving, I say, but she's exercising as well. Loosely put, the physical trainers attach electric wires to whatever muscles they can find on her body and jolt her with shocks that simulate running a steeplechase while being repeatedly struck by bolts of lightning. I say, It's very good for her body—terrible for her hair.

After that ordeal, my Miss Kathie is having her legs shaved, her teeth whitened, her cuticles pushed back.

Chewing, swallowing, **Terrence Terry** says, "Who's the new romance? Do I know him?"

The telephone mounted on the kitchen wall beside the stove, it rings. I lift the receiver, saying, Hello? And wait.

The front doorbell rings.

Over the telephone, a man's voice says, "Is Miss **Katherine Kenton** at home?"

Who, I ask, may I say is calling?

The front doorbell rings.

"Is this Hazie, the housekeeper?" the man on the telephone says. "My name is Webb Westward. We met a few days ago, at the mausoleum."

I'm sorry, I say, but I'm afraid he has the wrong number. This, I say, is the State Residence for Criminally Reckless Females. I ask him to please not telephone again. And I hang up the receiver.

"I see you're still," the Terrence specimen says, "protecting Her Majesty."

My pen follows the handwritten lines of the original letter, tracing every loop and dot of the words that bleed through, copying them onto this new sheet of stationery, the sentence: *My Most Dear Katherine, True love is NOT out of your reach.*

I trace the words, *I'll arrive to collect you for drinks at eight on Saturday.*

Tracing the line, *Wear something smashing.*

My pen traces the signature, **Webster Carlton Westward III.**

We all, more or less, live in her shadow. No matter what else we do with our lives, our obituaries will lead with the clause "lifelong paid companion to movie star **Katherine Kenton**" or "fifth husband to film legend **Katherine Kenton . . .**"

I copy the original letter perfectly, only instead of *Saturday* I mimic the handwriting, that same slant and angle, to write *Friday*. Folding this new letter in half, tucking it back into the original envelope with *Miss Katherine* written on the back, licking the glue strip, my tongue tastes the mouth of this Webster specimen. The lingering flavor of **Maxwell House coffee**. The scent of thin **Tiparillo** cigars and **bay rum** cologne. The chemistry of Webb Westward's saliva. The recipe for his kisses.

Terrence Terry sets the bag of candied almonds on the

kitchen table. Still eating one, he watches the television. He asks, "Where's that awful little mutt she picked up . . . what? Eight years ago?"

He's an actor now, I say, nodding at the television set. And it was ten years ago.

"No," says the Terrence specimen, "I meant the Pekingese."

I shrug, flip the dead bolt, slip the chain and open the door. I tell him the dog's still around. Probably upstairs napping. I say to leave the almonds, and I'll be certain that Miss Kathie gets them. Standing with the door open, I say good-bye.

On the television, Paco pretends to kiss **Vilma Bánky**. The senator on the evening news kisses babies and shakes hands. On another channel, **Terrence Terry** catches a bullet fired from a Union musket and dies at the **Siege of Atlanta**. We're all merely ghosts who continue to linger in Miss Kathie's world. Phantoms like the scent of honeysuckle or almonds. Like vanishing steam. The front doorbell rings again.

Taking the candy, I slip the forged love letter into the paper bag, where Miss Kathie will find it when she arrives home this afternoon, thoroughly shocked and shaved and ravenous.

ACT I, SCENE SEVEN

In the establishing shot, a taxicab stops in the street outside Miss Kathie's town house. Sunshine filters through the leaves of trees. Birds sing. The shot moves in, closer and closer, to frame an upstairs window, Miss Kathie's boudoir, where the drapes are drawn tight against the afternoon glare.

Inside the bedroom, we cut to a close-up shot of an alarm clock. Pull back to reveal the clock is balanced atop the stack of screenplays beside Miss Kathie's bed. On the clock, the larger hand sits at twelve, the smaller at three. Miss Kathie's eyes flutter open to the reflection of herself staring down, those same violet eyes, from the mirrors within her bed canopy. One languid movie star hand flaps and flops, stretching until her fingers find the water glass balanced beside the clock. Her fingers find the **Nembutal** and bring the capsule back to her lips. Miss Kathie's eyelashes flutter closed. Once more, the hand hangs limp off the side of her bed.

The forged version of the love letter, the copy I traced, sits in the middle of her mantelpiece, featured center stage among the lesser invitations and wedding photos. Among the polished awards and trophies. The original date, Saturday, revised to Friday, tonight. Here's the setup for a romantic evening that won't happen. No, **Webster Carlton Westward III** will not arrive at eight this evening, and **Katherine Kenton** will sit alone and fully dressed, coiffed, as abandoned as **Miss Havisham** in the novel by **Charles Dickens**.

Cut to a shot of the same taxicab as it pulls to the curb in front of a dry cleaner's. The back car door swings opens, and my foot steps out. I ask the cabdriver to double-park while I collect Miss Kathie's white sable from the refrigerated storage vault. The white fur folded over my arm, it feels impossibly soft but heavy, the pelts slippery and shifting within the thin layer of dry cleaner plastic. The sable glows with cold, swollen with cold in contrast to the warm daylight and the blistering, cracked-vinyl seat of the cab.

At our next stop, the dressmaker's, the cab stops for me to pick up the gown my Miss Kathie had altered. After that, we stop at the florist's to buy the corsage of orchids that Miss Kathie's nervous hands will fondle and finger tonight, as eight o'clock comes and goes and her brown-eyed young beau doesn't ring the doorbell. Before the clock strikes eight-thirty, Miss Kathie will ask me to pour her a drink. By the stroke of nine, she'll swallow a **Valium**. By ten o'clock, these orchids will be shredded. By then, my Miss Kathie will be drunken, despondent, but safe.

Our perspective cuts back and forth between the bedside alarm clock and the roving taxi meter. Dollars and minutes tick away. A countdown to tonight's disaster. We stop by the hairdresser's to collect the wig that's been washed and set. We stop by the hosier's for the waist cincher and a new girdle. The cobbler's, for the high heels Miss Kathie wanted resoled. The bodice of the evening gown feels crusted with beads and embroidery, rough as sandpaper or brick inside its garment bag.

The camera follows me, dashing about, assembling all the ingredients—breathless as a mad scientist or a gourmet chef—to create my masterpiece. My life's work.

If most American women imagine **Mary, Queen of Scots** or **the Empress Eugenie** or **Florence Nightingale**, they picture Miss Kathie in a period costume standing in a two-shot with **John Garfield** or **Gabby Hayes** on an **MGM** soundstage. In the public mind, Miss Kathie, her face and voice, is collapsed with the **Virgin Mary**, **Dolley Madison** and **Eve**, and I will not allow her to dissipate that legend. **William Wyler**, **C. B. DeMille** and **Howard Hawks** may have directed her in a picture or two, but I have directed Miss Kathie's entire adult life. My efforts have made her the heroine, the human form of glory, for the past three generations of women. I coached her to her greatest roles as **Mrs. Ivanhoe**, **Mrs. King Arthur** and **Mrs. Sheriff of Nottingham**. Under my tutelage, Miss Kathie will forever be synonymous with the characters of **Mrs. Apollo**, **Mrs. Zeus** and **Mrs. Thor**.

Now more than ever the world needs my Miss Kathie to personify their core values and ideals.

According to **Walter Winchell**, "menoposture" refers to the ramrod straight backbone of a **Joan Crawford** or an **Ethel Barrymore**, a lady of a certain age whose spine never touches the back of any chair. A **Helen Hayes**, who stands straight as a military cadet, her shoulders back in defiance of gravity and osteoporosis. That crucial age when older picture stars become what **Hedda Hopper** calls "fossilidealized," the living example of proper manners and discipline and self-restraint. Some **Katharine Hepburn** or **Bette Davis** illustration of noble hard work and Yankee ambition.

Miss Kathie has become the paragon I've designed. She illustrates the choice we must make between giving the impression of a very youthful, well-preserved older person, or appearing to be a very degraded, corrupt young person.

My work will not be distracted by some panting, clutching, brown-eyed male. I have not labored my entire lifetime to build a monument for idiot little boys to urinate against and knock down with their dirty hands.

The cab makes a quick stop at the corner newsstand for cigarettes. Aspirin. Breath mints.

In the same moment, the bedside clock strikes four, and the alarm begins to buzz. One long movie-star hand reaches, the fingers searching, the wrist and forearm clashing with gold bracelets and charms.

At the curb outside the town house, I'm passing a twenty-dollar bill to the cabdriver.

Inside, the alarm continues, buzzing and buzzing, until my own hand enters the shot, pressing the button, which ceases the noise. In addition to the wig and white sable, I've brought the gown, the corsage, the shoes. I've filled an ice bucket and brought clean towels and a bottle of chilled rubbing alcohol, everything as clean and sterile as if I were kneeling bedside to deliver a baby.

My fingers hold an ice cube, rubbing it in a slow arc below one violet eye to shrink Miss Kathie's loose skin. The ice skims over Miss Kathie's forehead, smoothing the wrinkles. The melting water saturates the skin of her cheeks, bringing pink to the surface. The cold shrinks the folds in her neck, drawing the skin tight along her jawline.

Our preparation for tonight, all of her rest and my work, as much fuss and sweat as my Miss Kathie would invest in any screen test or audition.

With one hand I'm blotting the melted water. Dabbing her face with cotton balls dipped in the cold rubbing alcohol, reducing the pores. Her skin now feels as frigid as the sable coat preserved in cold storage. At one time, every fur-bearing animal in the world lived in terror of **Katherine Kenton**. Like **Roz Russell** or **Betty Hutton**, if Miss Kathie chose to wear a coat of red ermine or a hat trimmed in pelican feathers, no ermine or seabird was safe. One photo of her arriving at an awards dinner or premiere was enough to put most animals onto the endangered species list.

This woman is **Pocahontas**. She is **Athena** and **Hera**. Lying in this messy, unmade bed, eyes closed, this is **Juliet Capulet**. **Blanche DuBois**. **Scarlett O'Hara**. With ministrations of lipstick and eyeliner I give birth to **Ophelia**. To **Marie Antoinette**. Over the next trip of the larger hand around the face of the bedside clock, I give form to **Lucrezia Borgia**. Taking shape at my fingertips, my touches of foundation and blush, here is **Jocasta**. Lying here, **Lady Windermere**. Opening her eyes, **Cleopatra**. Given flesh, a smile, swinging her sculpted legs off one side of the bed, this is **Helen of Troy**. Yawning and stretching, here is every beautiful woman across history.

My position is not that of a painter, a surgeon or a sculptor, but I perform all those duties. My job title: **Pygmalion**.

As the clock strikes seven, I'm hooking my creation into her girdle, lacing the waist cincher. Her shoulders shrug the gown over her head, and her hands smooth the skirts down each hip.

With the handle of a long rattail comb, I'm hooking and

tucking her gray hair into the edges of her auburn wig when Miss Kathie says, "Hush."

Her violet eyes jumping to the clock, she says, "Did you hear the doorbell just now?"

Still tucking away stray hairs, I shake my head, No.

When the clock strikes eight, the shoes are slipped onto her feet. The white sable draped across her shoulders. Her orchids, still chilled from the icebox, she cups them in her lap, sitting at the top of the stairs, looking down into the foyer, watching the street door. One diamond earring pushes forward, her head cocked to hear footsteps on the stoop. Maybe the muffled knock of a man's glove on the door, or the sound of the bell.

A whiskey later, Miss Kathie goes to the boudoir mantel and her violet eyes study the letter I forged. She takes the paper and holds it, sitting again on the stairs. Another whiskey later, she returns to her boudoir to fold the letter and tear it in half. She folds the page and tears it again, tears it again, and drops the fluttering pieces into the fireplace. The flames. One of my creations destroying another. My counterfeit **Medea** or **Lady Macbeth**, burning my false declaration of love.

True love is NOT out of your reach. Saturday replaced with Friday. Tomorrow, when **Webster Carlton Westward III** arrives for his actual dinner date, it will be too late to repair tonight's broken heart.

By a third whiskey, the orchids are worried and bruised to a pulp between Miss Kathie's fretting hands. When I offer to bring another drink, her face shines, sliced with the wet ribbons of her tears.

Miss Kathie looks down the stairs at me, blinking to dry her eyelashes, saying, "Realistically, what would a lovely young man like Webb want with an old woman?" Smiling at the crushed orchids in her lap, she says, "How could I be such a fool?"

She is no one's fool, I assure her. She's **Anne Boleyn** and **Marie Curie**.

Her eyes, in that scene, as dull and glassy as pearls or diamonds soiled with hair spray. In one hand, Miss Kathie balls the smashed flowers tight within her fist, to make a wad she drops into one empty old-fashioned glass. She hands the glass to me, the dregs of whiskey and orchids, and I hand her another filled with ice and gin. The sable coat slips from her shoulders to lie, heaped, on the stairway carpet. She's the infant born this afternoon in her bed, the young girl who dressed, the woman who sat down to wait for her new love. . . . Now she's become a hag, aged a lifetime in one evening. Miss Kathie lifts a hand, looking at her wrinkled knuckles, her marquise-cut diamond ring. Twisting the diamond to make it sparkle, she says, "What say we make a record of this moment?" Drive to the crypt beneath the cathedral, she means, and cut these new wrinkles into the mirror where her sins and mistakes collect. That etched diary of her secret face.

She draws her legs in close to her body, her knees pressed to her chest. All of her wadded as tight as the ruined fistful of flowers.

Throwing back a swallow of gin, she says, "I'm such an old ninny." She swirls the ice in the bottom of the glass, saying, "Why do I always feel so degraded?"

Her heart, devastated. My plan, working to perfection.

The rim of the glass, smeared red with her lipstick, the curved rim has printed her face with red, spreading the corners of her mouth upward to make a lurid clown's smile.

Her eyeliner dribbles in a black line down from the center of each eye. Miss Kathie lifts her hand, twisting the wrist to see her watch, the awful truth circled in diamonds and pink sapphires. Here's bad news presented in an exquisite package. From somewhere in the bowels of the town house, a clock begins to strike midnight. Past the twelfth stroke, the bell continues to thirteen, fourteen. More late than any night could possibly get. At the stroke of fifteen, my Miss Kathie looks up, her cloudy eyes confused with alcohol.

It's impossible. The bell tolling sixteen, seventeen, eighteen, it's the doorbell. And standing on the stoop, when I open the front door, there waits a pair of bright brown eyes behind an armful of roses and lilies.

ACT I, SCENE EIGHT

We open with a panning shot of Miss Kathie's boudoir mantel, the lineup of wedding photos and awards. Next, we dissolve to a similar panning shot, moving across the surface of a console table in her drawing room, crowded with more trophies. Then, we dissolve to yet another similar shot, moving across the shelves of her dining room vitrines. Each of these shots reveals a cluttered abundance of awards and trophies. Plaques and medals lie displayed in presentation boxes lined with white satin like tiny cradles, each medal hung on a wide ribbon, the box lying open. Like tiny caskets. Burdening the shelves are loving cups of tarnished silver, engraved, *To **Katherine Kenton**, In Honor of Her Lifetime Achievements, Presented by the **Baltimore Critics Circle**.* Statuettes plated with gold, from the **Cleveland Theater Owners Association**. Diminutive statues of gods and goddesses, tiny, the size of infants. *For Her Outstanding Contribution. For Her Years of*

Dedication. We move through this clutter of engraved bric-a-brac, these honorary degrees from Midwestern colleges. Such nine-carat-gold praise from the **Phoenix Stage Players Club**. The **Seattle Press Guild**. The **Memphis United Society of Thespis**. The **Greater Missoula Dramatics Community**. Frozen, gleaming, silent as past applause. The final panning shot ends as a dirty rag falls around one golden statue; then the camera pulls back to reveal me wiping the award free of dust, polishing it, and placing it back on the shelf. I take another, polish it and put it back. I lift another.

This demonstrates the endless nature of my work. By the time I've done them all, the first awards will need dusting and polishing. Thus I move along with my soiled cotton diaper, really the most soft kind of dust cloth.

Every month another group entices Miss Kathie to grace them with her presence, rewarding her with yet another silver-plate urn or platter, engraved, *Woman of the Year*, to collect dust. Imagine every compliment you've ever received, made manifest, etched into metal or stone and filling your home. That terrible accumulating burden of your Dedication and Talent, your Contributions and Achievements, forgotten by everyone except yourself. **Katherine Kenton**, the Great Humanitarian.

Throughout this sequence, always from offscreen, we hear the laughter of a man and woman. Miss Kathie and some famous actor. **Gregory Peck** or **Dan Duryea**. Her ringing laugh followed by his bass guffaw. As I'm dusting awards in the library of the town house, the laughter filters downstairs from her boudoir. If I'm working in the dining room, the laughter echoes from the drawing room. Nevertheless, when I follow the sound, any new room is empty. The laughter always comes from around another corner or from behind the next door. What I find are only the awards, turning dark with tarnish. Such honors—solid, worthless lead or pig iron merely coated with a thin skin of gold. After every rubbing, more dull, worn and smutty.

In her boudoir, on the television, my Miss Kathie rides in an open horse-drawn carriage through Central Park, sitting beside **Robert Stack**. Behind them trails a huge looming mass of white balloons. At a crescendo of violin music, Stack rolls on top of Miss Kathie, and her fist opens, releasing the frenzied balloons to scatter and swim upward, whipping their long tails of white string.

On some shelves balance scissors big enough for the **Jolly Green Giant**, brass buffed until it could pass as something precious, the pointed blades as long as Miss Kathie's legs. She brandished one pair to cut the ribbon at the opening ceremonies for the six-lane **Ochoakee Inland Expressway**. Another pair of scissors cut the ribbon to open the **Spring Water Regional Shopping Mall**. Another pair, as large as a golden child performing jumping jacks, these cut the ribbon at a supermarket. At the **Lewis J. Redslope Memorial Bridge**. At the **Tennessee** assembly plant for **Skyline Microcellular, Inc.**

On the television in the kitchen, Miss Kathie lies on a blanket next to **Cornel Wilde**. As Wilde rolls on top of her, the camera pans to a nearby spitting, crackling campfire.

Filling the shelves are skeleton keys so heavy they require both hands to lift. Tin treated to shine bright as platinum. Presented by the **Omaha Business Fathers** and the **Topeka Chamber of Commerce**. The key to **Spokane, Washington**, presented to Miss Kathie by his honor, the right esteemed **Mayor Nelson Redding**. The engraved keys to **Jackson Hole**,

Wyoming, and **Jacksonville, Florida**. The keys to **Iowa City** and **Sioux Falls**.

On the dining room television, my Miss Kathie shares a train compartment with **Nigel Bruce**. As he throws himself on top of her the train slips into a tunnel.

In the drawing room, **Burt Lancaster** lowers himself onto Miss Kathie as ocean waves roll onto a sandy beach. On the television in the den, **Richard Todd** throws himself onto Miss Kathie as July Fourth fireworks explode in a night sky.

Throughout this montage, the actual Miss Kathie is absent. Here and there, the camera might linger on a discarded newspaper page, a half-tone photograph of Miss Kathie exiting a limousine assisted by **Webster Carlton Westward III**. Her name in boldface type linked to his in the gossip columns of **Sheilah Graham** or **Elsa Maxwell**. Another photograph, the two of them dancing at a nightclub. Otherwise, the town house is empty.

My hand lifts still another trophy, a heroic statuette, the muscle of each arm and leg as small and naked as a child Miss Kathie never had, and I massage its face, without pressing, to make such thin gold, that faint shine, last as long as possible.

ACT I, SCENE NINE

"The most cunning compliments," playwright **William Inge** once wrote, "seem to flatter the person who bestows them even more than they do the person who receives them."

Once more we dissolve into flashback. Begin with a swish pan, fast enough to blur everything, then gradually slow to a long crane shot, swooping above round tables, each dinner table circled with seated guests. The gleam of every eye turns toward a distant stage; the sparkle of diamond necklaces and beaming, boiled-white tuxedo shirts reflect that far-off spotlight. We move through this vast field of white tablecloths and silverware as the shot advances toward the stage. Every shoulder turns, twisted to watch a man standing at a podium. As the shot comes into deep focus, we see the speaker, **Senator Phelps Russell Warner**, standing behind the microphone.

A screen fills the upstage wall, flashing with gray images

of a motion picture. For a few words, the figure of **Katherine Kenton** appears on-screen, wearing a corseted silk ball gown as **Mrs. Ludwig van Beethoven**. As her husband, **Spencer Tracy**, snores in the background, she hunches over a roll of parchment, quill pen squeezed between her blue fingers, finishing the score to his **Moonlight Sonata**. Her enormous face glowing, blindingly bright, from the silver-nitrate film stock. Her eyes flashing. Her teeth blazing white.

In the audience, every face is cast in chiaroscuro, half lost in the darkness, half lost in the glare of that distant light. Forgetting themselves outside of this moment, the audience sits aware only of the man onstage and his voice. Over all, we hear the rolling thunder of the senator's voice boosted through microphones, amplifiers, loudspeakers; this booming voice says, "She serves as our brilliant light, forever guiding forward the rest of us mortals. . . ."

Across the surface of the screen, we see my Miss Kathie in the role of **Mrs. Alexander Graham Bell**, elbowing her husband, **James Stewart**, aside so she can listen covertly to **Mickey Rooney** on their party line, wasp-waisted in a high-collar dress. Her Gibson-girl hair crowned with a picture hat of drooping egret plumes.

This, the year when every other song on the radio was **Doris Day** singing "Happiness Is Just a Thing Called Joe" backed by the **Bunny Berigan Orchestra**. In the audience, no single face draws our focus. Despite their pearls and bow ties, everyone looks plain as old character players, dress extras, happy to shoot a scene sitting down.

At the microphone, the senator continues, "Her sense of noble purpose and steadfast course of action sets the pattern for our highest aspirations. . . ." His voice sounds deep and steady as a **Harry Houdini** or a **Franz Anton Mesmer**.

This prattle, further example of what **Walter Winchell** means by the term "toast-masturbating." Or "laud mouthing," according to **Hedda Hopper**. According to **Louella Parsons**, "implying gilt."

Turning his head to one side, the senator looks off stage right, saying, "She visits our drab world like an angel from some future age, where fear and stupidity have been vanquished. . . ."

The camera follows his eye line to reveal Miss Kathie and myself standing in the wings, her violet eyes fixed on the senator's spotlighted figure. Him in his black tuxedo. Her in a white gown, one elbow bent to crush a pale hand to her heart. Cue the lighting change, bring down the key light, boost the fill light to isolate Miss Kathie in the wings. Block the scene with the senator as a groom, standing before a congregation, taking his vows prior to giving her some tin trophy painted gold in lieu of a wedding ring.

It's no wonder such bright lights seem invariably surrounded by the dried husks of so many suicidal insects.

"As a woman, she radiates charm and compassion," says the senator, his voice echoing about the hall. "As a person, she proves an eternal marvel." With each word, he climbs to her status, fusing himself to her name recognition and laying claim to the enormous dowry of her fame in his upcoming bid for reelection.

Upstage, the vast luminous face of my Miss Kathie hovers on-screen in the role of **Mrs. Claude Monet**, painting his famous water lilies. Her perfect complexion care of **Lilly Daché**. Her lips, **Pierre Phillipe**.

"She is the mother we wish we'd had. The wife we dream of finding. The woman whom all others measure themselves against," the senator says, shining and polishing Miss Kathie's image before the moment of her appearance. Before he presents her to this audience of the faithful. This stranger she's never met, coaxing her fans to a low-key frenzy of anticipation before she joins him in the spotlight.

More "projectile praise" and "force fawning" or "compliment vomit," in the eyes of **Cholly Knickerbocker**.

Everything sounds so much better when it comes out of a man's mouth.

Clasped in my hands, a screenplay rolled tight, here is the only prospect for work my Miss Kathie has been offered in months. A horror flick about an aged voodoo priestess creating an army of zombies to take over the world. At the finale, the female lead is dismembered, screaming, and eaten by wild monkeys. **Lynn Fontanne** and **Irene Dunne** have already passed on this project.

That trophy held by the senator, it will never shine as bright as it shines at this moment before it's received, while this object is still beyond Miss Kathie's grasp. From this distance apart, the senator and she both look so perfect, as if each offers the other some complete bliss. **Senator Phelps Russell Warner**, he's the stranger who would become her sixth "was-band." Himself a prize that seems worth the effort to dust and polish over the remainder of her lifetime.

Every coronation contains elements of farce. You must be a toothless, aged lion, indeed, before this many people will risk petting you. All of these tin-plate copies of **Kenneth Tynan**, trying to insist their opinions count for anything. Ridiculous clockwork copies of **George Bernard Shaw** and **Alexander Woollcott**. These failed actors and writers, a mob that's never created worthwhile art, they're now offering to carry the train of Miss Kathie's gown, hoping to hitch a ride with her to immortality.

Using a strong eye light, go to a medium close-up shot of Miss Kathie's face, her reaction, as the senator's off-camera voice says, "This woman offered the best of an era. She blazed paths where none had braved to venture. To her alone belong such memorable roles as **Mrs. Count Dracula** and **Mrs. President Andrew Jackson. . . .**"

Behind him play scenes from *The **Gene Krupa** Story* and *The Legend of **Genghis Khan***. Miss Katie, filmed in black and white, kisses **Bing Crosby** on a penthouse terrace overlooking a beautiful panoramic matte painting of the **Manhattan** skyline.

In the spotlight, the senator's florid, naked forehead shines as bright as the award. He stands tall, with wide shoulders tapering to his patent-leather shoes. A pink-flesh facsimile of the **Academy Award**. Above and behind his ears, the remainder of his hair retreats as if hiding from the crowd's attention. It's pathetic how easily a strong spotlight can wipe away any trace of a person's age or character.

It's this pink mannequin saying, "Hers is a beauty which will linger in the collective mind until the end of humanity; hers is a courage and intelligence which showcase the best of what human beings can accomplish. . . ."

By praising the frailty of this woman, the senator looks stronger, more noble, generous, loving, even taller and more grateful. This oversize man achieves a humility, fawning over this tiny woman. Such beautiful, false compliments—the male equivalent of a woman's screaming fake orgasm. The first designed to get a woman into bed. The second to more quickly complete sexual intercourse and get a man out of bed. As the senator says these words which every woman craves to hear, he evolves. His broad shoulders and thick neck of a caveman become those of a loving father, an ideal husband. A humble servant. This savage Neanderthal shape shifts. His teeth becoming a smile more than a snarl. His hairy hands tools instead of weapons.

"Tonight, we humbly beseech her to accept our admiration," says the senator, cradling the trophy in the crook of one arm. "But she is the prize which all men wish to win. She is the crowning jewel of our American theatrical tradition. So that we might give her our appreciation, ladies and gentlemen, may I give you . . . **Katherine Kenton.**"

Earning applause, not for any performance, but for simply not dying. This occasion, both her introduction to the senator and her wedding night.

I suppose it's a comfort, perhaps a sense of self-control, doing worse damage to yourself than the world will ever dare inflict.

Tonight, yet another foray into the great wasteland which is middle age.

Upon that cue, my Miss Kathie takes the spotlight, entering stage right to thunderous applause. More starved for applause than for any chicken dinner the occasion might offer. The scene shattered by the flash of hundreds of cameras. Smiling with her arms flung wide, she enters the senator's embrace and accepts that gaudy piece of gilded trash.

Coming out of the flashback, we slowly dissolve to a tight shot which reveals this same trophy, engraved, *From the Greater Inland Drama Maniacs of Western Schuyler County.* Over a decade later it sits on a shelf, the gold clouded with tarnish, the whole of it netted with cobwebs. A beat later a scrap of white cloth wraps the trophy; a hand lifts it from the shelf. With further pullback, the shot reveals me, dusting in the drawing room of the town house. Polishing. Stray spiderwebs cling to my face, and a halo of dust motes swirl around my head. Outside the windows, darkness. My gaze fixed on nothing one can actually see.

From offscreen, we hear a key turn in the lock of the front door. A draft of air stirs my hair as we hear the heavy door open and shut. The sound of footsteps ascending the main staircase from the foyer to the second floor. We hear a second door open and shut.

Abandoning the trophy, the dust cloth still in one hand, I follow the sound of footsteps up the stairs to where Miss Kathie's boudoir door is closed. A clock strikes two in some faraway part of the house as I knock at the door, asking if Miss Kathie needs help with her zipper. If she needs me to set out her pills. To draw her bath and light the candles on her fireplace mantel. The altar.

Through the boudoir door, no answer. When I grip the knob, it refuses to turn in either direction. Fixed. This door Miss Kathie has never locked. Pressing one dusty cheek to the wood, I knock again, listening. Instead of an answer, a faint sigh issues from inside. The sigh repeats, louder, then more loud, becoming the squeak of bedsprings. The only answer is that squeak of bedsprings, repeating, a squeak as high-pitched and regular as laughter.

ACT I, SCENE TEN

The scene opens with **Lillian Hellman** grappling in bare-handed combat with **Lee Harvey Oswald**, the two of them wrestling and punching each other near an open window on the sixth floor of the **Texas School Book Depository**, surrounded by prominent stacks of Hellman's *The Little Foxes* and *The Children's Hour* and *The Autumn Garden*. Outside the window, a motorcade glides past, moving through **Dealey Plaza**, hands waving and flags fluttering. Hellman and Oswald gripping a rifle between them, they yank the weapon back and forth, neither gaining complete control. With a violent head butt, slamming her blond forehead into Oswald's, leaving his eyes glazed and stunned for a beat, Hellman shouts, "Think, you commie bastard!" She screams, "Do you really want **LBJ** as your president?"

A shot rings out, and Hellman staggers back, clutching her shoulder where blood spouts in pulsing jets between her fingers. In the distance, the pink **Halston** pillbox hat of **Jacqueline Kennedy** moves out of firing range as we hear a second rifle shot. A third rifle shot. A fourth . . .

More rifle shots ring out as we dissolve to reveal the kitchen of **Katherine Kenton**, where I sit at the table, reading a screenplay titled *Twentieth Century Savior* authored by Lilly. Sunlight slants in through the alley windows, at a steep angle suggesting late morning or noontime. In the background, we see the servants' stairs, which descend from the second floor to the kitchen. The rifle shots continue, an audio bridge, now revealed to be the sound of footsteps coming down the stairs, the sound of the fantasy sequence bleeding into this reality.

As I sit reading, a pair of feet appear at the top of the servants' stairs, wearing pink mules with thick, heavy heels, *clop-clopping* lower down the stair steps to reveal the hem of a filmy pink dressing gown trimmed in fluttering pink egret feathers. First one bare leg emerges from the split in front, pink and polished from the ankle to the thigh; then the second leg emerges from the dressing gown, as the figure descends each step. The robe flapping around thin ankles. The steps continue, loud as gunshots, until my Miss Kathie fully emerges and stops in the doorway, slumped against one side of the door frame, her violet eyes half closed, her lips swollen, the lipstick smeared around her mouth from cheek to cheek, the red smeared from nose to chin, her face swooning in a cloud of pink feathers. Posed there, Miss Kathie waits for me to look up from the Hellman script, and only then does she waft her gaze in my direction and say, "I'm so happy not to be alone any longer."

Arrayed on the kitchen table are various trophies and awards, tarnished gold and silver, displaying different degrees

of dust and neglect. An open can of silver polish and a soiled buffing rag sit among them.

Clasping something in both hands, concealed behind her back, my Miss Kathie says, "I bought you a present . . ." and she steps aside to reveal a box wrapped in silver-foil paper, bound with a wide, red-velvet ribbon knotted to create a bow as big as a cabbage. The bow as deep red as a huge rose.

Miss Kathie's gaze wafts to the trophies, and she says, "Throw that junk out—please." She says, "Just pack them up and put them away in storage. I no longer need the love of every stranger. I have found the love of one perfect man. . . ."

Holding the wrapped package before her, offering the red-velvet-and-foil-wrapped box to me, Miss Kathie steps into the room.

On the scripted page, Lilly Hellman holds Oswald in a full nelson, both his arms bent and twisted behind his head. With one fast, sweeping kick, Lilly knocks Oswald's legs out from under him, and he crumbles to the floor, where the two grapple, scrabbling and clawing on the dusty concrete, both within reach of the loaded rifle.

Miss Kathie sets the package on the kitchen table, at my elbow, and says, "Happy birthday." She pushes the box, sliding it to collide with my arm, and says, "Open it."

In the Hellman script, Lilly brawls with superhuman effort. The silence of the warehouse broken only by grunts and gasps, the grim sound of struggle in ironic contrast to the applause and fanfare, the blare of marching bands and the blur of high-stepping majorettes throwing their chrome batons to flash and spin in the hard **Texas** sunshine.

Not looking up from the page, I say it isn't my birthday.

Looking from trophy to trophy, my Miss Kathie says, "All of this 'Lifetime Achievement . . .'" Her hand dips into an invisible pocket of her dressing gown and emerges with a comb. Drawing the comb through her dyed-auburn hair, a fraction, only a day or two of gray showing at the roots, drawing the comb away from her scalp, Miss Kathie lets the long strands fall, saying, "All this 'Lifetime Contribution' business makes me sound so—dead."

Not waiting for me, Miss Kathie says, "Let me help." And she yanks at the ribbon.

With a single pull, the lovely bow unravels, and my Miss Kathie wads up the silver paper, tearing the foil from the box. Inside the box, she uncovers folds of black fabric. A black dress with a knee-length skirt. Layered beneath that, a bib apron of starched white linen, and a small lacy cap or hat stuck through with hairpins.

The smell of her hair, on her skin, a hint of **bay rum**, the cologne of **Webster Carlton Westward III**. **Paco** wore **Roman Brio**. The senator wore **Old Lyme**. Before the senator, "was-band" number five, **Terrence Terry**, wore **English Leather**. The steel tycoon wore **Knize** cologne.

Leaving the dress on the table, Miss Kathie crosses stage right still combing her hair, to where she stands on her pink-mule toes to reach the television atop the icebox. The screen flares when she flips the switch and the face of **Paco Esposito** takes form, as gradual as a fish appearing beneath the surface of a murky pond. The male equivalent of a diamond necklace, a stethoscope, hangs around his neck. A surgical mask is bunched under his chin. Still gripping a bloody scalpel, Paco is snaking his tongue down the throat of an ingénue, **Jeanne Eagels**, dressed in a red-and-white-striped uniform.

"I don't want the placement agency getting any idea

that you're more than a servant," says my Miss Kathie. She cranks the dial switch one click to another television station, where **Terrence Terry** dances lead for the **Lunenburg battalion** against **Napoleon** at the **Battle of Mont St. Jean.** Still drawing the comb through her hair, Miss Kathie clicks to a third station, where she appears, **Katherine Kenton** herself, in black and white, playing the mother of **Greer Garson** in the role of **Louisa May Alcott** opposite **Leslie Howard** in a biopic about **Clara Barton.**

She says, *bark, oink, cluck* . . . **Christina** and **Christopher Crawford.**

"Nothing," says Miss Kathie, "makes a woman look younger than holding her own precious newborn."

Cluck, buzz, bray . . . **Margot Merrill.**

Another click of the television reveals Miss Kathie made up to be an ancient mummy, covered in latex wrinkles and rising from a papier-mâché sarcophagus covered with hieroglyphics to menace a screaming, dewy **Olivia de Havilland.**

I ask, Newborn *what?*

Hoot, tweet, moo . . . **Josephine Baker** and her entire **Rainbow Tribe.**

In a tight insert shot we see the reveal: the dress, there on the kitchen table, this gift, it's strewn with long, auburn hairs, that heavy mahogany color that hair has only when it's soaking wet. The discarded wrapping paper, the ribbon and comb, left for me to pick up. The black dress, it's a housemaid's uniform.

My position in this household is not that of a mere maid or cook or lady-in-waiting. I am not employed in any capacity as domestic help.

This is not a birthday present.

"If the agency asks, I think maybe you'll be an au pair,"

Miss Kathie says, standing on tiptoe, her nose near her own image on the television screen. "I love that word . . . *au pair*," she says. "It sounds almost like . . . French."

In the screenplay, Lilly Hellman looks on in horror as **President John F. Kennedy** and **Governor John Connally** explode in fountains of gore. Her arms straight at her sides, her hands balled into fists, Lilly throws back her head, emptying her mouth, her throat, emptying her lungs with one, long, howling, "Noooooooooooooo . . . !" The rigid silhouette of her pain outlined against the wide, flat-blue **Dallas** sky.

I sit staring at the wrinkled uniform, the torn wrapping paper. The stray hairs. The screenplay laid open in my lap.

"You can bring up the coffee in a moment," says Miss Kathie, as she shuts off the television with a slap of her palm. Gripping the skirt of her gown and lifting it, she crosses stage right to the kitchen table. There, Miss Kathie plucks the lacy cap from the open box, saying, "In the future, Mr. Westward prefers cream in his coffee, not milk."

Placing the white cap on the crown of my head, she says, "*Voilà!*" She says, "It's a perfect fit." Pressing the lacy cap snug, Miss Kathie says, "That's Italian for *prego*."

On my scalp, a sting, the faint prick of hairpins feel sharp and biting as a crown of thorns. Then a slow fade to black as, from offscreen, we hear the front doorbell ring.

ACT I, SCENE ELEVEN

If you'll permit me to break character and indulge in another aside, I'd like to comment on the nature of equilibrium. Of balance, if you'd prefer. Modern medical science recognizes that human beings appear to be subject to predetermined, balanced ratios of height and weight, masculinity and femininity, and to tinker with those formulas brings disaster. For example, when **RKO Radio** and **Monogram** and **Republic Pictures** began prescribing injections of male hormones in order to coarsen some of their more effete male contract players, the inadvertent result was to give those he-men breasts larger than those of **Claudette Colbert** and **Nancy Kelly**. It would seem the human body, when given additional testosterone, increases its own production of estrogen, always seeking to return to its original balance of male and female hormones.

Likewise, the actress who starves herself to far, far below her natural body weight will soon balloon to far above it.

Based on decades of observation, I propose that sudden high levels of external praise always trigger an equal amount of inner self-loathing. Most moviegoers are familiar with the theatrically unbalanced mental health of a **Frances Farmer**, the libidinal excesses of a **Charles Chaplin** or an **Errol Flynn**, and the chemical indulgences of a **Judy Garland**. Such performances are always so ridiculously broad, played to the topmost balcony. My supposition is that, in each case, the celebrity in question was simply making adjustments—instinctually seeking a natural equilibrium—to counterbalance enormous positive public attention.

My vocation is not that of a nurse or jailer, nanny or au pair, but during her periods of highest public acclaim, my duties have always included protecting Miss Kathie from herself. Oh, the overdoses I've foiled . . . the bogus land investment schemes I've stopped her from financing . . . the highly inappropriate men I've turned away from her door . . . all because the moment the world declares a person to be immortal, at that moment the person will strive to prove the world wrong. In the face of glowing press releases and reviews the most heralded women starve themselves or cut themselves or poison themselves. Or they find a man who's happy to do that for them.

For this next scene we open with a beat of complete darkness. A black screen. For the audio bridge, once more we hear the ring of the doorbell. As the lights come up, we see the inside of the front door, and from within the foyer, we see the shadow of a figure fall on the window beside the door, the shape of someone standing on the stoop. In the bright crack of sunlight under the door we see the twin shadows of two feet shifting. The bell rings again, and I enter the shot, wearing the black dress, the maid's bib-front apron and lacy white cap. The bell rings a third time, and I open the door.

The foyer stinks of paint. The entire house stinks of paint.

A figure stands in the open doorway, backlit and over-exposed in the glare of daylight. Shot from a low angle, the silhouette of this looming, luminous visitor suggests an angel with wings folded along its sides and a halo flaring around the top of its head. In the next beat, the figure steps forward into the key light. Framed in the open doorway stands a woman wearing a white dress, a short white cape wrapped around her shoulders, white orthopedic shoes. Balanced on her head sits a starched white cap printed with a large red cross. In her arms, the woman cradles an infant swaddled in a white blanket.

This beaming woman in white, holding a pink baby, appears the mirror opposite of me: a woman dressed in black holding a bronze trophy wrapped in a soiled dust rag. A beat of ironic parallelism.

A few steps down the porch stands a second woman, a nun shrouded in a black habit and wimple, her arms cradling a babe as blond as a miniature **Ingrid Bergman**. Its skin as clear as a tiny **Dorothy McGuire**. What **Walter Winchell** calls a "little bundle of goy."

On the sidewalk stands a third woman, wearing a tweed suit, her gloved fingers gripping the handle of a perambulator. Sleeping inside the pram, two more infants.

The nurse asks, "Is **Katherine Kenton** at home?"

Behind her, the nun says, "I'm from St. Elizabeth's."

From the sidewalk, the woman wearing tweed says, "I'm from the placement agency."

At the curb, a second uniformed nurse steps out of a taxicab carrying a baby. From the corner, another nurse approaches with a baby in her arms. In deep focus, we see a second nun advancing on the town house, bearing yet another pink bundle.

From offscreen we hear the voice of Miss Kathie say, "You've arrived. . . ." And in the reverse angle we see her descending the stairs from the second floor, a housepainter's brush in one hand, dripping long, slow drops of pink paint from the bristles. Miss Kathie's rolled back the cuffs of her shirt, a man's white dress shirt, the breast pocket embroidered with *O.D.*, the monogram for her fourth "was-band," **Oliver "Red" Drake, Esq.**, all of the shirt spotted with pink paint. A bandanna tied to cover her hair, and pink paint smudged on the peak of one movie-star cheekbone.

The town house stinks of lacquer, choking and acrid as a gigantic manicure compared to the smell of talcum powder and sunlight on the doorstep.

Miss Kathie's feet descend the last steps, trailed by drops of pink. Her blue denim dungarees, rolled halfway up to her knees, reveal white bobby socks sagging into scuffed penny loafers. She faces the nurse, her violet eyes twitching between the gurgling, pink orphan and the paintbrush in her own hand. "Here," she says, "would you mind . . . ?" And my Miss Kathie thrusts the brush, slopping with pink paint, into the nurse's face.

The two women lean together, close, as if they were kissing each other's cheeks, trading the swaddled bundle for the brush. The white uniform of the nurse, spotted with

pink from touching Miss Kathie. The nurse left holding the gummy pink brush.

Her arms folded to hold the foundling, Miss Kathie steps back and turns to face the full-length mirror in the foyer. Her reflection that of **Susan Hayward** or **Jennifer Jones** in *Saint Joan* or *The Song of Bernadette*, a beaming **Madonna** and child as painted by **Caravaggio** or **Rubens**. With one hand, my Miss Kathie reaches to the nape of her own neck, looping a finger through the knot of the bandanna and pulling it free from her head. As the bandanna falls to the foyer floor, Miss Kathie shakes her hair, twisting her head from side to side until her auburn hair spreads, soft and wide as a veil, framing her shoulders, the white shirt stretched over her breasts, framing the tiny newborn.

"Such a pièce de résistance," Miss Kathie says, rubbing noses with the little orphan. She says, "That's the Italian word for . . . *gemütlichkeit*."

Miss Kathie's violet eyes spread, wide-open, bug-eyed as **Ruby Keeler** playing a virgin opposite **Dick Powell** under the direction of **Busby Berkeley**. Her long movie-star hands, her cheeks marred only by the pastel stigmata of pink paint. Her eyes clutching at the image in the foyer mirror, Miss Kathie turns three-quarters to the left, then the right, each time closing her eyelids halfway and nodding her head in a bow. She bows once more, facing the mirror full-on, her smile stretching her face free of wrinkles, her eyes glowing with tears. This, the exact same performance Miss Kathie gave last month when she accepted the lifetime tribute award from the **Denver Independent Film Circle**. These identical gestures and expressions.

A beat later, she unloads the infant, returning the bundle

to the nurse, Miss Kathie shaking her head, wrinkling her movie-star nose and saying, "Let me think about it. . . ."

As the nun mounts the porch steps, Miss Kathie thrusts two fingers into her own dungarees pocket and fishes out a card of white paper. . . . She holds the sample shade of **Honeyed Sunset** to the cherub's pink cheek, studying the card and the infant together. Shaking her head with a flat smile, she says, "Clashes." Sighing, Miss Kathie says, "We've already painted the trim. Three coats." She shrugs her movie-star shoulders and tells the nun, "You understand. . . ."

The next newborn, Miss Kathie leans close to its drowsing face and sniffs. Using an atomizer, she spritzes the tender lips and skin with **L'air du Temps** and the tiny innocent begins to squall. Recoiling, Miss Kathie shakes her head, No.

Another gurgling newborn, Miss Kathie leans too close and the dangling hot ash drops off the tip of her cigarette, resulting in a flurry of tiny screams and flailing. The smell of urine and scorched cotton. As if a pressing iron had been left too long on a pillowcase soaked in ammonia.

Another foundling arrives barely a shade too pale for the new nursery drapes. Holding a fabric swatch beside the squirming bundle, Miss Kathie says, "It's almost **Perfect Persimmon** but not quite **Cherry Bomb**. . . ."

The doorbell rings all afternoon. All the day exhausted with "offspring shopping," as **Hedda Hopper** calls it. "*Bébé* browsing," in the semantics of **Louella Parsons**. A steady parade of secondhand urchins and unwanted *kinder*. A constant stream of arriving baby nurses, nuns and adoption agents, each one blushing and pop-eyed upon shaking the pink, paint-sticky hand of Miss Kathie. Each one babbling: *Tweet, cluck, hoot* . . . **Raymond Massey**. A quick-cut montage.

Bray, bark, buzz . . . **James Mason.**

Another nurse retreats, escaping down the street when Miss Kathie asks how difficult it might be to dye the hair and diet some pounds off of a particularly rotund cherub.

Another social worker flags a taxicab after Miss Kathie smears a tiny foundling with **Max Factor** base pigment, ladies' foundation number six.

Pursing her lips, she hovers over the face of one wee infant, saying, "*Wunderbar* . . ." Exhaling cigarette smoke to add, "That's the Latin equivalent for *que bueno*."

Miss Kathie brandishes each child in the foyer mirror, hefting it and cuddling its pinched little face, studying the effect as if each orphan were a new purse or a stage prop.

Meow, squawk, squeak . . . **Janis Paige.**

Another tiny urchin, she leaves smudged with lipstick.

Another, Miss Kathie leans too close, too quickly, splashing a newborn with the icy-cold **Boodles** gin of her martini.

Another, she frowns down upon while her long, glossy fingernails pick at a mole or flaw on its smooth, pink forehead. "As the Spanish would say . . ." she says, "*qué será será*."

This "*kinder* kattle kall,*" as **Cholly Knickerbocker** would call it, continues all afternoon. This audition. Prams and strollers form a line which runs halfway to the corner. This buffet of abandoned babies, the products of unplanned pregnancies, the progeny of heartbreak—these pink and chubby souvenirs of rape, promiscuity, incest. Impulse. Bottle-fed leftovers of divorce, spousal abuse and fatal disease. Even as the paintbrush, the pink bristles grow stiff in my hand, the babies arrive as proof of poor choices. The sleeping or giggling flotsam and jetsam, a residue of what seemed at one time to be true love.

Each innocent, Miss Kathie holds, modeling it for the

foyer mirror. Doing take after take of this same scene. Giving her right profile, her left. Smiling full-face, then fluttering her eyelashes, ducking her movie-star chin, emoting in reaction shots, telling the mirror, "Yes, she *is* lovely. I'd like you to meet my daughter: Katherine Jr."

Telling the mirror, "I'd like to introduce my son, **Webster Carlton Westward the Fourth.**" She repeats this same line of dialogue with each child before handing it back to the nurse, the nun, the waiting social worker. Comparing paint chips and fabric samples. Picking over each child for scars or defects. And for every infant Miss Kathie sends away, two more arrive to stand in line for a test.

Into the late afternoon, she's reciting: *Bark, cluck, bray* . . . **Katherine Kenton, Jr.**

Oink, quack, moo . . . **Webster Carlton Westward IV.**

She performs take after take, hours of that same screen test, until the streetlights flicker and blink, flare and shine bright. From the avenue, the sound of traffic fades. Across the street, in the windows of town houses, the curtains slide closed. Eventually Miss Kathie's front steps descend to the sidewalk, empty of orphans.

In the foyer, I stoop to retrieve the bandanna dropped on the floor. The fallen drops of pink paint, smeared and dry, form a fading pink path, a stream of pink spots tracked down the steps, down the street. A trail of the rejected.

A taxicab pulls to a stop at the curb. The driver opens his door, steps out and unlocks the trunk. He removes two suitcases and places them on the sidewalk, then opens the back door of the cab. A foot emerges, a man's shoe, the cuff of a trouser leg. A man's hand grips the door of the cab, a signet ring glinting gold around the little finger. A head of hair emerges from the backseat of the cab, eyes bright brown as root beer. A smile flashes, bright as July Fourth fireworks.

A specimen boasting the wide shoulders of **Dan O'Herlihy**, the narrow waist of **Marlon Brando**, the long legs of **Stephen Boyd**, the dashing smile of **Joseph Schildkraut** playing **Robin Hood**.

In the reverse angle, my Miss Kathie rushes to the front door, calling, "Oh, my darling . . ." Her outstretched arms and thrusting bosom at once a suggestion of **Julie Newmar** playing **Penelope** greeting **Odysseus**. **Jane Russell** in the role of **Guinevere** reunited with **Lancelot**. **Carole Lombard** rushing to embrace **Gordon MacRae**.

Webster Carlton Westward III calls up the steps, noble as **William Frawley** as **Romeo Montague**, "Kath, my dearest . . ." Calling, "Do you have three dollars to pay the cabdriver?"

The driver, standing beside the suitcases, stoic as **Lewis Stone**, gristled as **Fess Parker**. The cab itself, yellow.

Her auburn hair streaming behind her, Miss Kathie shouts, "Hazie!" She calls, "Hazie, take Mr. Westward's luggage to my room!" The two brazen lovers embrace, their lips meeting, while the camera circles and circles them in an arch shot, dissolving to a funeral.

ACT I, SCENE TWELVE

Act one, scene twelve opens with another flashback. Once more, we dissolve to **Katherine Kenton** cradling a polished cremation urn in her arms. The setting: again, the dimly lit interior of the Kenton crypt, dressed with cobwebs, the ornate bronze door unlocked and swung open to welcome mourners. A stone shelf at the rear of the crypt, in deep shadow, holds various urns crafted from bronze, copper, nickel. The urn in her arms, engraved, *Oliver "Red" Drake, Esq.*, Miss Kathie's fifth "was-band."

This took place the year when every other song on the radio was **Frank Sinatra** singing the **Count Basie** arrangement of "**Bit'n the Dust.**"

My Miss Katie hugs the urn, lifting it to meet the black lace of her veiled face. Behind the veil, her lips. She plants a puckered lipstick kiss on the engraved name, then places this new urn on the dusty shelf among the others. Amidst the bottles of brandy and **Luminal**. The unlit prayer candles. The only other cast members in this three-shot, myself and **Terrence Terry**, each of us prop Miss Kathie by one elbow. What **Louella Parsons** would call "pal bearers."

The collection of crematory urns stand among dusty bottles and magnums of champagne. Vessels of the living and the dead, stacked here in the chilled, dry dark. Miss Kathie's entire cellar, stored together. The urns stand. The bottles lie on their sides, all of them netted and veiled with cobwebs.

Bark, oink, squeal . . . **Dom Pérignon 1925.**

Bark, meow, bray . . . **Bollinger 1917.**

Terrence Terry peels the gilded lead from the cork of one bottle. He twists the loop, loosening the wire harness which holds the mushroom cork in the mouth of the bottle. Holding the bottle high, pointed toward an empty corner of the crypt, Terry pries at the cork with both his thumbs until the pop echoes, loud inside the stone room, and a froth of foam gushes from the bottle, spattering on the floor.

Roar, cluck, whinny . . . **Perrier-Jouët.**

Tweet, quack, growl . . . **Veuve Clicquot.**

That **Tourette's syndrome** of brand names.

Terry lifts a champagne glass from the stone shelf, holding the bowl of the glass near his face and pursing his lips to blow dust from it. He hands the glass to Miss Kathie and pours it full of champagne. A ghost of cold vapor rises from and hovers around the open bottle.

With each of us holding a dusty glassful of champagne, Terry lifts his arm in a toast. "To Oliver," he says.

Miss Kathie and myself, we lift our glasses, saying, "To Oliver."

And we all drink the sweet, dirty, sparkling wine.

Buried in the dust and cobwebs, the mirror lies facedown

in its silver frame. Following a moment of silence, I lift the mirror and lean it to stand against the wall. Even in the dim light of the crypt, the scratches sparkle on the glass surface, each etched line the record of a wrinkle my Miss Kathie has had stretched or lifted or burned away with acid.

Miss Kathie lifts her veil and steps to her mark, the lipstick X on the stone floor. Her face in perfect alignment with the history of her skin. The gray hairs gouged into the mirror align with her hair. She pinches the fingertips of one black glove, using her opposite hand, tugging until the glove slides free. Miss Kathie twists the diamond engagement ring and the wedding band, handing the diamond to me, and placing the gold band on the dusty shelf beside the urns. Beside the urns of past dogs. Beside past shades of lipstick and fingernail varnish too bright, deemed too young for her to wear any longer.

Each of the various champagne glasses, set and scattered within the crypt, cloudy with dust and past wine, the rim of each glass is a museum of different lipstick shades Miss Kathie has left behind. The floor, littered with the butts of ancient cigarettes, some filters wrapped with these same ancient colors of lipstick. All these abandoned drinks and smokes set on ledges, on the floor, tucked into stony corners, this setting like an invisible cocktail party of the deceased.

Watching this, our ritual, Terry dips a hand into the inside pocket of his suit coat. He plucks out a chrome cigarette case and snaps it open, removing two cigarettes, which he places, together, between his lips. Terry flicks a flame to jump from one corner of the chrome case, and lifts it to light both cigarettes. With a snap of his wrist, the flame is gone, and Terry replaces the thin case, returned to inside his coat. He plucks one cigarette from his mouth, trailing a spiral of smoke, and reaches to place it between the red lips of Miss Kathie.

This flashback takes place before the crow's-feet caused by **Paco Esposito**. Before I scratched the frown lines related to the senator into this mirror of **Dorian Gray**.

Wielding the diamond, I get to work drawing. I trace any new wrinkles, adding any new liver spots to this long-term record. Sketching the network of tiny spider veins puckered around the filter of Miss Kathie's burning cigarette.

Terry says, "A word of warning, Lady Kath." Sipping his filthy champagne, he says, "If you'll take my advice. You need to be careful. . . ."

As Terry explains, too many lady stars in her situation have opened their doors to a young man or a young woman, someone who'd sit and listen and laugh. The rapt attention might last for a year or a month, but eventually the young admirer would disappear, returning to another life among people his own age. The young woman would marry and vanish with her own first child, leaving the actress, once more, abandoned. On occasion a letter might arrive, or a telephone call. Keeping tabs.

In the same manner **Truman Capote** kept in touch with **Perry Smith** and **Dick Hickock** while they sat on death row. Biding his time. Capote needed a finale for *In Cold Blood*.

Every major publisher in America harbors a book, the advance money already paid to some pleasant young person, a handsome, affable listener, who'd spun a few evenings of dinner into a movie-star tell-all biography and needed only a cause of death to complete the final chapter. Already, that pack of stage-door hyenas waited on **Mae West** to die. They phoned **Lelia Goldoni**, hoping for bad news. Scanned the obituary pages for **Hugh Marlowe**, **Emlyn Williams**, **Peggie Castle** and **Buster Keaton**. Vultures circling. Most were already finagling introductions to **Ruth Donnelly** and **Geraldine Fitzgerald**. At this moment, they sit in front of a fireplace in the parlor of **Lillian Gish** or **Carole Landis**, vacuuming up the thorny anecdotes they'd need to flesh out two hundred pages, their vulture eyes committing to memory every gesture of **Butterfly McQueen**, every tic or mannerism of **Tex Avery** that could be sold to the ravenous reading public.

All of those future best-selling books, they were already typeset, merely waiting for someone to die.

"I know you, Kath," says Terry, turning his head to blow smoke. The stale air of the crypt heavy with the smell of smoke and mold. He takes the wedding ring from the dusty stone shelf, saying, "I know you're a sucker for an audience, even an audience of one."

Some grocery delivery boy or a girl conducting a door-to-door survey . . . these ambitious stray dogs, they each sit *clack-clacking* on a rusty typewriter at home. A pretty, wide-eyed, starstruck youngster will steal Miss Kathie's life story. Her reputation. Her dignity. Then pray for her to die.

With the diamond, I cut the furrows of sadness across her forehead. Updating Miss Kathie's life story. The map of her. The mirror already scratched with years of worry and grief and scars documenting Miss Kathie's secret face.

Judy Garland, Terry says, and **Ethel Merman** never again walked out, not in public, not with as much of their previous pride and glamour, after **Jacqueline Susann** cast them as the fat, drunken, foulmouthed characters **Neely O'Hara** and **Helen Lawson** in *The Valley of the Dolls*.

In response, the diamond shrieks against the glass. The high-pitched, wailing sound of funeral keening.

Dropping to one knee on the cold stone floor, Terry looks up at Miss Kathie and says, "Will you marry me? Just to keep you safe?" He reaches out to take her hand. He says, "At least until something better comes along?"

This, a sodomite and a faded movie star, is what **Walter Winchell** calls a "match made in resignation." Terry proposes becoming her emotional bodyguard, a live-in placeholder between real men.

"Just like your portrait here," says Terry, nodding at the mirror in its silver frame, "any friendly young biographer is only going to showcase your flaws and faults in order to build his own career."

As always, I drag the diamond in straight lines to mimic the tears running down Miss Katie's face.

I shake my head, Don't. Don't let's repeat this torture. Don't trust another one.

As always, another duty of my job is to never press too hard lest the mirror shatter.

My Miss Kathie slips a hand into the slit of one fur coat pocket, fishing out something pink she sets on the dusty shelf. Exhaling cigarette smoke, she says, "I guess I won't be needing this. . . ." So many years ago, this something Miss Kathie meant to leave behind forever.

It was her diaphragm.

Terry slips the wedding band onto her finger.

Miss Kathie smiles, saying, "It still feels warm." She adds, "The *ring*, not the *diaphragm*."

And I pour everyone another round of champagne.

ACT I, SCENE THIRTEEN

The scene opens with a tight shot of **John Glenn** strapped into the astronaut seat within the capsule of the *Friendship 7* spacecraft, the first American to orbit **Earth**. Beyond the capsule's small window we see our glorious blue planet swirled with white clouds, suspended among the pinprick stars in the deep blackness of space. As Glenn's gloved hands fiddle with the wide assortment of controls on the panel before him, flipping a switch, turning a knob, he leans into a microphone, saying, "Mission control, I think we might have a problem. . . ."

Glenn says, "Mission control, do you read me?" He says, "I seem to be losing power. . . ."

In unison, every light on the control panel blinks out. The lights blink on for a moment, then off. Flickering, the lights go out altogether, leaving Glenn in only the faint glow of the stars. Seated in absolute silence, Glenn wraps both gloved hands around the microphone, bringing his mouth almost to touch the wire mesh of it and shouting, "Please, **Houston!**" Screaming, "**Alan Shepard**, you bastard, don't let me die up here!"

The shot pulls back to reveal an interior panel in the wall behind Glenn's astronaut chair. A handle in the center of the panel begins to slowly turn. Drawing focus because it's the only movement in the shot, highlighted by a key light in the otherwise murky compartment.

Glenn quietly sobs in the darkness.

Insert a close-up of the handle turning, intercutting with extreme close-ups of Glenn's face, his sobs and tears fogging the inside surface of his helmet face shield.

From offscreen, we hear a familiar voice say, "Pipe down."

In a medium shot, we see the panel behind Glenn swing open, revealing a stowaway **Lillian Hellman** as she steps free from what appears to be a storage locker. In one continuous shot, she steps through a doorway, under a stenciled sign reading, WARNING: AIR LOCK. Hellman says, "Wish me luck, you big baby." She draws a deep breath, and her hand slaps a large, red button labeled, JETTISON. An inner door slides shut, sealing the air lock, and a burst of mist belches Lilly from the side of the orbiting capsule. She wears no helmet, no pressurized suit, only an elegant sports ensemble of slacks and sweater designed by **Adrian**.

Weightless and floating in the black void of outer space, Lilly swims, holding her breath. Her arms stroke, and her legs kick in an Australian crawl, inching her way along the side of the orbiting space capsule until she arrives beside a small tin-colored box affixed to the outer hull. The box is stenciled, SOLAR MODULE, and it flashes with an occasional burst of bright sparks. Still holding her breath, her cheeks inflated and her brow furrowed in concentration, Lilly drags a ball-peen hammer from the hip pocket of her slacks ensemble accessorized with **Orry-Kelly** high heels. Her chandelier earrings and turquoise squash-blossom pendant are still tethered to Lilly, but float and drift in the absence of gravity. Gripping the hammer in her blue fingers, the veins swelling under the skin at her temples, Lilly swings the steel head to collide with the module box. In the vacuum of space, we hear nothing, only silence and the steady *thump-thump* of Lilly's enormous heart beating faster and faster. The hammer strikes the module a second time. Sparks fly. The tin-colored metal dents, and flakes of gray paint float away from the point of impact.

More hammer blows fall; with each the sound rings louder, then louder as we dissolve to reveal the kitchen of **Katherine Kenton**, where I sit at the kitchen table, reading a screenplay titled *Space Race Rescue* penned by Lilly. I wear the black maid's uniform, over it the bib apron. On my head the starched, lacy maid's cap. The hammer blows continue, an audio bridge, now revealed to be an actual pounding sound coming from within the town house.

The blows ring more loud, more fast as we cut to a shot of the bed headboard in Miss Kathie's boudoir, revealing the sounds as the headboard pounding the wall. The sexual coupling takes place below the bottom of the frame, barely outside the shot, but we can hear the heavy breathing of a man and a woman as the tempo and volume of the pounding increase. Each impact makes the framed paintings jump on the walls. The curtain tassels dangle and dance. The bedside pile of screenplays slumps to the floor.

On the page, as Lilly's astronaut heart beats faster and

her hammer batters the box again and again, we hear the headboard of Miss Kathie's bed slamming the wall, faster, until with one final, heroic pounding, the lights of the space module flicker back to life. The pounding ceases as all the various gauges and dials flare back to full power and, framed in the module's little window, **John Glenn** gives Lilly the thumbs-up. Tears of horror and relief stream down the face inside his astronaut helmet.

In the background of the kitchen, two hairy feet appear at the top of the servants' staircase, two hairy ankles descend from the second floor, two hairy knees, then the hem of a white terry-cloth bathrobe. Another step down, and the cloth belt appears, tied around a narrow waist; two hairy hands hang on either side. A chest appears, the terry cloth embroidered with a monogram: *O.D.* The robe of the long-deceased fourth "was-band." Another step reveals the face of **Webster Carlton Westward III**. Those bright brown root-beer eyes. A smile parts his face, pulling at the corners of his mouth, spreading them like a stage curtain, and this American specimen says, "Good morning, Hazie."

On the page, Lilly Hellman struggles in the cold, black void of space, dragging herself along the hull of the *Friendship 7*, fighting her way back to the air lock.

The Webster specimen opens a kitchen cabinet and collects the percolator. He pulls out a drawer and retrieves the power cord. He does each task on his first attempt, without hunting. He reaches into the icebox without looking and removes the metal can of coffee grounds. From another cabinet, he takes the morning tray—not the silver tea tray nor the dinner tray. It's clear he knows what's what in this household and where each item is hidden.

This **Webster C. Westward III** appears to be a quick study. One of those clever, smiling young men **Terrence Terry** warned my Miss Kathie about. Those jackals. A magpie.

Spooning coffee grounds into the percolator basket, the Webster specimen says, "If you'll permit me to ask, Hazie, do you know whom you remind me of?"

Without looking up from the page, Lilly suffocating in the freezing stratosphere, I say, **Thelma Ritter**.

I was **Thelma Ritter** before **Thelma Ritter** was **Thelma Ritter**.

To see how I walk, watch **Ann Dvorak** walk across the street in the film *Housewife*. You want to see me worried, watch how **Miriam Hopkins** puckers her brow in *Old Acquaintance*. Every hand gesture, every bit of physical business I ever perfected, some nobody came along and stole. **Pier Angeli**'s laugh started out as my laugh. The way **Gilda Gray** dances the rumba, she swiped it from me. How **Marilyn Monroe** sings she got by hearing me.

The damned copycats. There's worse that people can steal from you than money.

Someone steals your pearls and you can simply buy another strand. But if they steal your hairstyle, or the signature manner in which you throw a kiss, it's much more difficult to replace.

Back a long time ago, I was in motion pictures. Back before I met up with my Miss Kathie.

Nowadays, I don't laugh. I don't sing or dance. Or kiss. My hair styles itself.

It's like **Terrence Terry** tried to warn Miss Kathie: the whole world consists of nothing but vultures and hyenas wanting to take a bite out of you. Your heart or tongue or violet eyes. To eat up just your best part for their breakfast.

You want to see **Tallulah Bankhead,** not just her playing **Julie Marsden** in *Jezebel,* or being **Regina Giddens** in *The Little Foxes,* but the real Tallulah, you only need to watch **Bette Davis** in *All About Eve.* It was **Joseph L. Mankiewicz** who wrote **Margo Channing** based on his poor mother, the actress **Johanna Blumenau,** but it was Davis who cozied up to Tallulah long enough to learn her mannerisms. Tallulah's delivery and how she walked. How she'd enter a room. The way Tallulah's voice got screechy after one bourbon. How, after four of them, her eyelids hung, half closed as steamed clams.

Of course, not everybody was in on the joke. It could be some **Andy Devine** or **Slim Pickens** farmers in **Sioux Falls** couldn't see Davis doing a minstrel-show version of Tallulah, but everybody else saw. Imagine a real performer watching you drink at a hundred parties, memorizing you while you're upset and spitting in the face of **William Dieterle,** then making you into a stage routine and performing you for the whole world to laugh at. The same as how that big shit **Orson Welles** made fun of **Willy Hearst** and poor **Marion Davies.**

The Webster specimen holds the percolator in the sink, filling it with water from the faucet. He assembles the basket, the spindle and the lid, plugs the female end of the electric cord into the percolator base and plugs the male end into the power socket.

Folks in **Little Rock** and **Boulder** and **Budapest,** most folks don't know what's not true. That bunch of **Chill Wills** rubes. So the whole entire world gets thinking that cartoon version Miss Davis created is the real you.

Bette Davis built her career playing that burlesque version of **Tallulah Bankhead.**

Nowadays, if anybody mentions poor **Willy Hearst,** you

picture Welles, fat and shouting at **Mona Darkfeather**, chasing **Peel Trenton** down some stairs. For anybody who never shook hands with Tallulah, she's that bug-eyed harpy with that horrid fringe of pale, loose skin flapping along Davis's jawline.

It boils down to the fact that we're all jackals feeding off each other.

The percolator pops and snaps. A splash of brown coffee perks inside the glass bulb on top. A wisp of white steam leaks from the chrome spout.

The Webster specimen's got it backward, I tell him. **Thelma Ritter** is a copy of me. Her walk and her diction, her timing and delivery, all of it was coached. At first **Joe Mankiewicz** turned up everywhere. I might sit down to dinner next to **Fay Bainter**, across the table from **Jessie Matthews**, who only went anywhere with her husband, **Sonnie Hale**, next to him **Alison Skipworth**, on my other side **Pierre Watkin**, and Joe would be way up above the salt, not talking to anyone, never taking his eyes off me. He'd study me like I was a book or a blueprint, his diseased fingers bleeding through the tips of his white gloves.

In his movie, **Thelma Ritter** wearing those cardigan sweaters half unbuttoned with the sleeves pushed back to the elbow, that was me. Thelma was playing me, only bigger. Hammy. My same way of parting my hair down the middle. Those eyes that follow every move at the same time. Not many folks knew, but the folks I knew, *they* knew. My given name is Hazie. The character's called Birdie. Mankiewicz, that rat bastard, he wasn't fooling anyone in our crowd.

It's like seeing **Franklin Pangborn** play his fairy hairdresser. **Al Jolson** in blackface. Or **Everett Sloane** doing his hook-nosed-Jew routine. Except this two-ton joke lands on only you, you don't share the load with nobody else, and folks expect you to laugh along or you're being a poor sport.

If you need more convincing, tell me the name of the broad who sat for **Leonardo da Vinci's** painting the **Mona Lisa.** People remember poor **Marion Davies,** and they picture **Dorothy Comingore,** drinking and hunched over those enormous **Gregg Toland** jigsaw puzzles on an **RKO** soundstage.

You talk about art imitating life, well, the reverse is true.

On the scripted page, **John Glenn** creeps down the outside of the space capsule hull, embracing Lilly Hellman and pulling her to safety. Inside the window of the orbiting capsule, we see them kissing passionately. We hear the buzz of a hundred zippers ripping open and see a flash of pink skin as they tear the clothes from each other. In zero gravity, Lilly's bare breasts stand up, firm and perfect. Her purple nipples erect, hard as flint arrowheads.

In the kitchen, the Webster specimen places the percolator on the morning tray. Two cups and saucers. The sugar bowl and creamer.

When I met her, Kathie Kenton was nothing. A Hollywood hopeful. A hostess in a steakhouse, handing out menus and clearing dirty plates. My job is not that of a stylist or press agent, but I've groomed her to become a symbol for millions of women. Across time, billions. I may not be an actor, but I've created a model of strength to which women can aspire. A living example of their own incredible possible potential.

Sitting at the table, I reach over and take a silver teaspoon from one saucer. With the spoon bowl cupped to my mouth,

I exhale moist breath to fog the metal. I lower the spoon to the hem of my lacy maid's apron and polish the silver between folds of the fabric.

In the Hellman screenplay, through the window of the space capsule we see Lilly's bare neck and shoulders arch with pleasure, the muscles rippling and shuddering as Glenn's lips and tongue trail down between her floating, weightless breasts. The fantasy dissolves as their panting breath fogs the window glass.

Buffing the spoon, I say, "Please don't hurt her. . . ." Placing the spoon back on the tray, I say, "I'll kill you before I'll let you hurt Miss Kathie."

With two fingers I pluck the starched white maid's cap from my head, the hairpins pulling stray hairs, plucking and tearing away a few long hairs. Rising to my feet, I reach up with the cap between my hands, saying, "You're not as clever as you think, young man," and I set the maid's cap on the very tip-top of this Webster's beautiful head.

ACT I, SCENE FOURTEEN

Cut to me, running, a trench coat worn over my maid's uniform flapping open in front to reveal the black dress and white apron within. In a tracking shot, I hurry along a path in the park, somewhere between the dairy and the carousel, my open mouth gasping. In the reverse angle, we see that I'm rushing toward the rough boulders and outcroppings of the **Kinderberg** rocks. Matching my eye line, we see that I'm focused on a pavilion built of brick, in the shape of a stop sign, perched high atop the rocks.

Intercut this with a close-up shot of the telephone which sits on the foyer table of Miss Kathie's town house. The telephone rings.

Cut to me running along, my hair fluttering out behind my bare head. My knees tossing the apron of my uniform into the air.

Cut to the telephone, ringing and ringing.

Cut to me veering around joggers. I'm dodging mothers pushing baby carriages and people walking dogs. I jump dog leashes like so many hurdles. In front of me, the brick pavilion atop **Kinderberg** looms larger, and we can hear the nightmarish calliope music of the nearby carousel.

Cut to the foyer telephone as it continues to ring.

As I arrive at the brick pavilion, we see an assortment of people, almost all of them elderly men seated in pairs at small tables, each pair of men hunched over the white and black pieces of a chess game. Some tables sit within the pavilion. Some tables outside, under the overhang of its roof. This, the chess pavilion built by **Bernard Baruch**.

Cut back to the close-up of the foyer telephone, its ringing cut off as fingers enter the shot and lift the receiver. We follow the receiver to a face, my face. To make it easier, picture **Thelma Ritter**'s face answering the telephone. In this intercut flashback we watch me say, "Kenton residence."

Still watching me, my reaction as I answer the telephone, we hear the voice of my Miss Kathie say, "Please come quick." Over the telephone, she says, "Hurry, he's going to kill me!"

In the park, I weave between the tables shared by chess players. On the table between most pairs sits a clock displaying two faces. As each player moves a piece, he slaps a button atop the clock, making the second hand on one clock face stop clicking and making the other second hand begin. At one table, an old-man version of **Lex Barker** tells another old **Peter Ustinov**, "Check." He slaps the two-faced clock.

Seated at the edge of the crowd, my Miss Kathie sits alone at a table, the top inlaid with the white and black squares of a chessboard. Instead of pawns, knights and rooks, the table holds only a thick ream of white paper. Both her hands clutch the stack of paper, as thick as the script for a **Cecil B. DeMille** epic. The lenses of dark sunglasses hide her violet eyes. A silk **Hermès** scarf, tied under her chin, hides her movie-star profile. Reflected in her glasses, we see two of me approach. Twin **Thelma Ritters**.

Sitting opposite her at the table, I say, "Who's trying to kill you?"

Another ancient **Slim Summerville** moves a pawn and says, "Checkmate."

From the offscreen distance, we hear the filtered ambient noise of horse carriages clip-clopping along the Sixty-fifth Street Traverse. Taxicabs honk on Fifth Avenue.

Miss Kathie shoves the ream of paper, sliding it across the chessboard toward me. She says, "You can't tell anyone. It's so humiliating."

Bark, oink, screech . . . **Screen Star Stalked by Gigolo**.

Moo, meow, buzz . . . **Lonely, Aging Film Legend Seduced by Killer**.

The stack of papers, she says she discovered them while unpacking one of Webb's suitcases. He's written a biography about their romantic time together. Miss Kathie pushes the stack at me, saying, "Just read what he says. . . ." Then immediately pulling the pages back, hunching her shoulders over them and glancing to both sides, she whispers, "Except the parts about me permitting Mr. Westward to engage me in anal intercourse are a complete and utter fabrication."

An aged version of **Anthony Quinn** slaps a clock, stopping one timer and starting another.

Miss Kathie slides the pages within my reach, then pulls them back, whispering, "And just so you know, the scene where I perform oral sex on Mr. Westward's person in the toilet of **Sardi's** is also a total bold-faced lie. . . ."

She looks around again, whispering, "Read it for yourself,"

pushing the stack of pages across the chessboard in my direction. Then, yanking the pages back, she says, "But don't you believe the part where he writes about me under the table at **Twenty-one** doing that unspeakable act with the umbrella. . . ."

Terrence Terry predicted this: a handsome young man who would enter Miss Kathie's life and linger long enough to rewrite her legend for his own gain. No matter how innocent their relationship, he'd merely wait until her death so he could publish his lurid, sordid tale. No doubt a publisher had already given him a contract, paid him a sizable advance of monies against the royalties of that future tell-all best seller. Most of this dreadful book was in all probability already typeset. Its cover already designed and printed. Once Miss Kathie was dead, someday, the tawdry lies of this charming parasite would replace anything valuable she'd accomplished with her life. The same way **Christina Crawford** has forever sullied the legend of **Joan Crawford**. The way **B. D. Merrill** has wrecked the reputation of her mother, **Bette Davis**, and **Gary Crosby** has dirtied the life story of his father, **Bing Crosby**—Miss Kathie would be ruined in the eyes of a billion fans.

The type of tome **Hedda Hopper** always calls a "lie-ography."

Around the chess pavilion, a breeze moves through the maple trees, making a billion leaves applaud. A withered version of **Will Rogers** reaches his old **Phil Silvers** hand to nudge a white king forward one square. Near us, an aged **Jack Willis** touches a black knight and says, "*J'adoube.*"

"That's French," Miss Kathie says, "for *tout de suite.*"

Shaking her head over the manuscript, she says, "I wasn't snooping. I was only looking for some cigarettes." My Miss Kathie shrugs and says, "What can we do?"

It's not libel until the book is published, and Webb has no intention of doing that until she's dead. After that, it will be his word against hers—but by then, my Miss Kathie will be packed away, burned to ash and interred with **Loverboy** and **Oliver "Red" Drake, Esq.**, and all the empty champagne bottles, the dead soldiers, within her crypt.

The solution is simple, I tell her. All Miss Kathie needs to do is live a long, long life. The answer is . . . to simply not die.

And pushing the manuscript pages across the chessboard, shoving them at me, Miss Kathie says, "Oh, Hazie, I wish it were that simple."

Printed, centered across the title page, it says:

Love Slave: A Very Intimate Memoir of
My Life with Kate Kenton

Copyright and author,
Webster Carlton Westward III

This is no partial story, says Miss Kathie. This draft already includes a final chapter. Pulling the ream of paper back to her side of the table, she flips over the stack of pages and turns the last few faceup. Near the ending, her voice lowered to a faint whisper, only then does she begin to read aloud, saying, " 'On the final day of Katherine Kenton's life, she dressed with particular care. . . .' "

As old men slap clocks to make them stop.

My Miss Kathie whispers to me the details about how, soon, she would die.

ACT II, SCENE ONE

Katherine Kenton continues reading as voice-over. At first we continue to hear the sounds of the park, the *clip-clopping* of horse-drawn carriages and the calliope music of the carousel, but these sounds gradually fade. At the same time we dissolve to show Miss Kathie and **Webster Carlton Westward III** lounging in her bed. In voice-over we still hear Miss Kathie's voice reading, an audio bridge from the preceding scene: " '. . . On the final day of **Katherine Kenton**'s life, she dressed with particular care.' "

Reading from the "lie-ography" written by Webb, the voice-over continues, " 'Our lovemaking felt more poignant. Seemingly for no special reason the muscles of her lovely, seasoned vagina clung to the meaty shaft of my love, milking the last passionate juices. A vacuum, like some haunting metaphor, had already formed between our wet, exhausted surfaces, our mouths, our skin and privates, requiring an extra force of effort for us to tear ourselves asunder.' "

Continuing to read from the final chapter of *Love Slave*, Miss Kathie's voice-over says, " 'Even our arms and legs were reluctant to unknot themselves, to untangle from the snarl of moistened bedclothes. We lay glued together by the adhesive qualities of our spent fluids. Our shared being pasted into becoming a single living organism. The copious secretions held us as a second skin while we embraced in the lingering ebb of our sensuous copulations.' "

Through heavy star filters, the boudoir scene appears hazy. Almost as if dense fog or mist fills the bedroom. Both lovers move in dreamy slow motion. After a beat, we see that the bedroom is Miss Kathie's but the man and woman are younger, idealized versions of Webster and Katherine. Like dancers, they rise and groom—the woman brushing her hair and rolling stockings up her legs, the man popping his cuffs, inserting cuff links, and brushing lint from his shoulders— with the exaggerated, stylized gestures of **Agnes de Mille** or **Martha Graham**.

Miss Kathie's voice, reading, says, " 'Only the beckoning prospect of dinner reservations at the **Cub Room**, a shared repast of **lobster thermidor** and **steak Diane** in the scintillating company of **Omar Sharif**, **Alla Nazimova**, **Paul Robeson**, **Lillian Hellman** and **Noah Beery** coaxed us to rise and dress for the exciting evening ahead.' "

As the voice-over continues, the lovers dress. They seem to orbit each other, continuing to fall into each other's embrace, then straying apart.

" 'Donning a **Brooks Brothers** double-breasted tuxedo,' " the voice-over reads, " 'I could envision an infinite number of such evenings stretching into our shared future of love. Leaning close to tie my white bow tie, Katherine said, "You have the largest, most gifted penis of any man alive." I recall the moment distinctly.' "

The voice-over continues, " 'Inserting a white orchid in my buttonhole, Katherine said, "I would die without you plumbing my salty depths."

" 'In retrospect, I think,' " Miss Kathie's voice-over says, " ' "If only that were true." ' "

As the idealized Katherine and Webster caress each other, the voice-over says, " 'I fastened the back of her enticing **Valentino** frock, offering my arm to guide her from the bedchamber, down the steps of her elegant residence to the busy street, where I might engage a passing conveyance.' "

The idealized lovers seem to float from the boudoir down the town house stairs, hand in hand, floating through the foyer and down the porch steps to the sidewalk. In contrast to their languid movements, the street traffic rushes past with ominous roars, motortrucks and taxicabs, blurred with speed.

" 'As the stream of vehicles whizzed past us,' " the voice-over reads, " 'almost invisible in their high velocity, I sank to one knee on the curb.' "

The idealized Webb kneels before the idealized Miss Kathie.

" 'Taking her limpid hand, I ask if she—the most glorious queen of theatrical culture—would consider wedding me, a mere presumptuous mortal. . . .' "

In soft-focus slow motion, the idealized Webb lifts the hand of the idealized Katherine until the long, smooth fingers meet his pursed lips. He plants a kiss on the fingers, the back of the hand, the palm.

The voice-over continues, " 'At that moment of our tremendous happiness, my beloved Katherine—the only great ideal of the twentieth century—stumbled from the treacherous curbstone . . .' "

In real time, we see the flash of a chrome bumper and radiator grille. We hear brakes screech and tires squeal. A scream rings out.

" '. . . falling,' " the voice-over reads, " 'directly into the deadly path of a speeding omnibus.' "

Still reading from *Love Slave*, Miss Kathie's voice-over says, " 'The end.' "

Bark, moo, meow . . . **Final curtain.**

Growl, roar, oink . . . **Fade to black.**

ACT II, SCENE TWO

Webb planned to kill her on this night. Tonight they had dinner reservations at the **Cub Room** with **Alla Nazimova, Omar Sharif, Paul Robeson** and . . . **Lillian Hellman.** Their plans had been to spend the afternoon together, dress late and catch a taxicab to the restaurant. Miss Kathie hands me the manuscript, telling me to sneak it back to its hiding place in Webb's suitcase, under his shirts, but on top of his shoes, tucked tight into one corner.

This scene begins with a very long shot of the chess pavilion atop the **Kinderberg** rocks. From this distance my Miss Kathie and I appear as two minute figures wandering down a path from the pavilion, dwarfed by the background of skyscrapers, lost in the huge landscape, but our voices sounding distinct and clear. Around us, a hush has fallen over the din and sirens of the city.

Walking in the distance, the pair of us are distinct as the

only two figures that remain together. Always in the center of this very, very long shot. Around us, single, distant figures jog, skate, stroll, but Miss Kathie and I move across the visual field at the same even pace, two dots traveling in a straight line as if we were a single entity, walking in identical slow strides. In tandem. Our steps the same length.

As our twin pinprick figures cross the wide shot, Miss Kathie's voice says, "We can't go to the police."

In response, my voice asks, Why not?

"And we mustn't mention this to anyone in the press, either," says Miss Kathie.

Her voice continues, "I will not be humiliated by a scandal."

It's not a crime to write a story about someone's demise, she says, especially not a movie star, a public figure. Of course, Miss Kathie could file a restraining order alleging Webb had abused her or made threats, but that would make this sordid episode a matter of public record. An aging film queen suckered into dyeing her hair, dieting and nightclub hopping, she'd look like the doddering fool from the **Thomas Mann** novella.

Even if Webb didn't, the tabloids would slay her.

She and I, almost invisible in the distance, continue to move through the width of this long, long shot. Around us the park drops into twilight. Still, the paired specks of us move at the same steady speed, no more fast or more slow. As we walk, the camera tracks, always keeping us at the very center of the shot.

A clock chimes seven times. The clock tower in the park zoo.

The dinner reservations are for eight o'clock.

"Webb has written the whole dreadful book," says the

voice of Miss Kathie. "Even if I confront him, even if I avoid tonight's conspiracy, his plot might not end here."

Among the ambient background sounds, we hear a passing bus, a roaring reminder of my Miss Kathie being crushed to bloody sequins. Possibly only an hour or two from now. Her movie-star auburn hair and perfect teeth, white and gleaming as the dentures of **Clark Gable**, would be lodged in a grinning chrome radiator grille. Her violet eyes would burst from their painted sockets and stare up from the gutter at a mob of her appalled fans.

The evening grows darker as our tiny figures move toward the edge of the park, nearing Fifth Avenue. At one instant, all the streetlights blink on, bright.

In that same instant, one tiny figure stops walking while the second figure takes a few more steps, moving ahead.

The voice of Miss Kathie says, "Wait." She says, "We have to see where this is going. We'll have to read the second draft and the third and the fourth drafts, to see how far Webb will go to complete his awful book."

I must sneak this draft back into his suitcase, and every day, as Miss Kathie foils each subsequent murder attempt, we need to look for the next draft so we can anticipate the next plot. Until we can think of a solution.

As the traffic light changes, we cross Fifth.

Cut to the pair of us approaching Miss Kathie's town house, a medium shot as we ascend the front steps to the door. From the street, in the second-floor window of her boudoir, we see that a hairy hand holds the curtains open a crack and bright brown eyes watch us arrive. From within the house, we hear footsteps thunder down the stairs. The front door swings open, and Mr. Westward stands in the light of the foyer. He wears the double-breasted **Brooks**

Brothers tuxedo cited in the last chapter of *Love Slave*. An orchid in his lapel buttonhole. The two ends of a white bow tie hang, looped and loose around his collar, and **Webster Carlton Westward III** says, "We'll need to hurry to stay on schedule." Looking down on us, he holds each end of his tie and leans forward, saying, "Would it kill you to help me with this?"

Those hands, the soft tools he would use to commit murder. Behind that smile, the cunning mind that had planned this betrayal. To add insult to injury, the lies he'd written about my Miss Kathie and her sexual adventures, they would eventually be cherry-picked by **Frazier Hunt** of *Photoplay*, **Katherine Albert** of *Modern Screen* magazine, **Howard Barnes** of the *New York Herald Tribune*, **Jack Grant** of *Screen Book*, **Sheilah Graham**, all the various low-life bottom feeders of *Confidential* and every succeeding biographer of the future. These tawdry, soft, sordid fictions would petrify and fossilize to become diamond-hard, carved-stone facts for all perpetuity. A salacious lie will always trump a noble truth.

Miss Kathie's violet eyes waft to meet my eyes.

A bus roars past in the street, shaking the ground with its weight and trailing the stink of diesel exhaust. Around us the air swirls, gritty with dust and heavy with the threat of imminent death.

Then Miss Kathie steps up to the stoop where the Webster specimen waits. Standing on her tiptoes, she begins to knot the white bow tie. Her movie-star face a mere breath from his own. For this moment and for the immediate future, placing herself as far as possible from the constant, marauding stream of omnibuses.

And Webb, the evil, lying bastard, looks down and plants a kiss on her forehead.

ACT II, SCENE THREE

We cut to the interior of a lavish Broadway theater. The opening mise-en-scène includes the proscenium arch, the stage curtain rising within the arch, below that the combed heads and brass instruments of musicians within the orchestra pit. The conductor, **Woody Herman**, raises his baton, and the air fills with a rousing overture by **Oscar Levant**, arrangements by **André Previn**. Additional musical numbers by **Sigmund Romberg** and **Victor Herbert**. On the piano, **Vladimir Horowitz**. As the curtain rises, we see a chorus line which includes **Ruth Donnelly, Barbara Merrill, Alma Rubens, Zachary Scott** and **Kent Smith** doing fan kicks aboard the deck of the battleship USS *Arizona*, designed by **Romain de Tirtoff** and moored center stage. The Japanese admirals **Isoroku Yamamoto** and **Hara Tadaichi** are danced by **Kinuyo Tanaka** and **Tora Teje**, respectively. **Andy Clyde** does a furious buck-and-wing as Ensign **Kazuo Sakamaki**, the official

first Japanese prisoner of war. **Anna May Wong** tap-dances a solo in the part of Captain **Mitsuo Fuchida**, and **Tex Ritter** fills in for General **Douglas MacArthur**. With **Emiko Yakumo** and **Tia Xeo** as Lieutenant Commander **Shigekazu Shimazaki** and Captain **Minoru Genda**, the principal dancers among the Japanese junior officers.

Choreography by *moo, cluck, bark* . . . **Léonide Massine**.

Staging by *tweet, bray, meow* . . . **W. MacQueen Pope**.

As the orchestra pounds away, the USS *Oklahoma* explodes near the waterline and begins to sink stage right. Burning fuel oil races stage left, moving upstage to ignite the USS *West Virginia*. Downstage, a Japanese **Nakajima** torpedo lances into the hull of the USS *California*.

Japanese **Zeros** strafe the production number, riddling the chorus line with bullets. **Aichi** dive bombers plunge into **Pearl White** and **Tony Curtis**, prompting an explosion of red corn syrup, while the cruising periscopes of Japanese midget submarines cut back and forth behind the footlights.

As the *Arizona* begins to keel over, we see **Katherine Kenton** clamber to the position of port-side gun, wrestling the body of a dead gunner's mate away from the seat. Embroidered across one side of her chest, the olive-drab fabric reads: PFC HELLMAN. My Miss Kathie drags the dead hero aside, laying both her palms open against his chest. As grenades explode shrapnel around her, Miss Kathie's lips mutter a silent prayer. The eyelids of the dead sailor, played by **Jackie Coogan**, the eyelashes flutter. The young man opens his eyes, blinking; cradled now in Miss Kathie's arms, he looks up into her famous violet eyes and says, "Am I in heaven?" He says, "Are you . . . God?"

The Zeros screaming past, the *Arizona* sinking beneath them into the oily, fiery water of **Pearl Harbor**, Miss Kathie laughs. Kissing the boy on his lips, she says, "Close but no cigar . . . I'm **Lillian Hellman**."

Before another note from the orchestra, Miss Kathie leaps to slam an artillery round into the massive deck gun. Wheeling the enormous barrel, she tracks a diving Aichi bomber, aligning the crosshairs of her gun sight. Her sailor whites artfully stained and shredded by **Adrian Adolph Greenberg**, her bleeding wounds suggested by sparkling patches of crimson sequins and rhinestones sewn around each bullet hole. Singing the opening bars of her big song, Miss Kathie fires the shell, blasting the enemy aircraft into a blinding burst of papier-mâché.

From offscreen a voice shouts, "Stop!" A female voice shouts, cutting through the violins and French horns, the rockets and machine-gun fire, shouting, "For fuck's sake, stop!" A woman comes stomping down the center aisle of the theater, one arm lifted, wielding a script rolled as tight as a police officer's billy club.

The orchestra grinds to silence. The singers stop, their voices trailing off. The dancers slow to a standstill, and the fighter jets hang, stalled, limp in midair, from invisible wires.

From the stage apron, in the reverse angle, we see this shouting woman is **Lillian Hellman** herself as she says, "You're ruining history! For the love of **Anna Q. Nilsson**, I happen to be *right-handed*!"

In this same reverse angle, we see that the theater is almost empty. **King Vidor** and **Victor Fleming** sit in the fifth row with their heads huddled together, whispering. Farther back, I sit in the empty auditorium next to **Terrence Terry**, both of us balancing infants on our respective laps. Clustered on the floor around our chairs, other foundlings squirm and drool in wicker baskets. Chubby pink hands shake various rattles, these *kinder* occupying most of the surrounding seats.

"You'd better hope this show flops," says **Terrence Terry**, bouncing a gurgling orphan on his knee. "By the way, where is our lethal Lothario?"

I tell him that Webb would have to truly hate Miss Kathie after what happened yesterday.

Onstage, Lilly Hellman shouts, "Everybody, listen! Let's start over." Hellman shouts, "Let's take it from the part where the **kamikaze** fighters of the **Japanese Imperial Army** swoop low over **Honolulu** in order to rain their deadly fiery cargo of searing death on **Constance Talmadge**."

The Webster specimen is currently undergoing treatment at **Doctors Hospital**. Just to escape the town house, Miss Kathie's going into rehearsal, and **Webster Carlton Westward III** is recovering from minor lacerations to his arms and torso.

Terry says, "Fingernail scratches?"

At the house, I say, the nurses keep arriving. The nuns and social workers. The fresh castoff infants continue to be delivered, and Miss Kathie declines to choose. In the past few days, each baby seems less like a blessing and more like an adorable time bomb. No matter how much you love and cuddle one, it still might grow up to become **Mercedes McCambridge**. Regardless of all the affection you shower on a child, it still might break your heart by becoming **Sidney Skolsky**. All of your nurturing and worry and careful attention might turn out another **Noel Coward**. Or saddle humanity with a new **Alain Resnais**. You need only look at Webb and see how no amount of Miss Kathie's love will redeem him.

Wrapped around one wrist, the foundling I hold wears a

beaded bracelet reading, UNCLAIMED BOY INFANT NUM-BER THIRTY-FOUR.

It's ludicrous, the idea of me raising a child, not while I still have my Miss Kathie to parent. A baby is such a blank slate, like training the understudy for a role you're planning to leave. You truly hope your replacement will do the play justice, but in secret you want future critics to say you played the character better.

"Don't look at me," Terry says, juggling an orphan. "I'm busy trying to raise myself."

Despite repeatedly sidestepping possible death by bus accident and dinner at the Cub Room with Lilly Hellman, Miss Katie has invited Webb to share her town house—so that we might better monitor future drafts of his book-in-progress. She confessed, knowing now how Webster was actually a psychotic killer, a ruthless scheming slayer, now their sex life was more passionate than ever.

It was Webb who brought this stage project to Miss Kathie, gave her the script to read and told her she'd be ideal as the brash, ballsy Hellman seduced by **Sammy Davis Jr.** and parachuted onto **Waikiki Beach** with nothing but a bottle of sunblock and orders to stem the Imperial Army's advance. Along the way she falls in love with **Joi Lansing**. According to Webb, this starring role had **Tony Award** written all over it.

According to **Terrence Terry**, the Webster specimen was merely grooming my Miss Kathie. These past few years, she'd fallen into obscurity. First, refusing stage and film projects. Second, neglecting her gray hair and weight. A generation of young people were growing up never hearing the name **Katherine Kenton**, oblivious to Miss Kathie's body of work.

No, it wouldn't do for her to die at this point in time, not before she'd made a successful comeback. Therefore, **Webster Carlton Westward III** coaxed her to slim down; in all likelihood he'd bully her into a surgeon's office, where she'd submit to having any new wrinkles or sags erased from her face.

If this new show was a hit, if it put my Miss Kathie back on top, introducing her to a new legion of fans, that would be the ideal time to complete his final chapter. His "lieography" would hit stores the same day her newspaper obituary hit the street. The same week her new Broadway show opened to rave reviews.

But not this week, I tell Terry.

Daubing with the hem of my starched maid's apron, I wipe at the face of the infant I hold. I lean near the floor and pick out a thin sheaf of papers tucked beneath the diaper of a nearby baby. Offering the printed pages to Terry, I ask if he wants to read the second draft of *Love Slave*. Just the closing chapter; here's the blueprint for Miss Kathie's most recent brush with death.

"How is it our homicidal hunk has landed himself in the hospital?" Terry says.

And I toss the newest, revised final chapter at his feet.

Onstage, Lilly demonstrates to Miss Kathie the correct way to *tour en l'air* while slitting the throat of an enemy sentry.

Terry collects the pages. Still holding the orphan on his knee, he says, "Once upon a time . . ." He props the baby in the crook of one arm, leaning into its tiny face as if it were a radio microphone or a camera lens, any recording device in which to store his life. Speaking into this particular foundling, filling its hollow mind, filling its eyes and ears with the sound of his voice, Terry reads, " 'Perhaps it's ironic, but no film critic, not **Jack Grant** nor **Pauline Kael** nor **David Ogden Stewart**, would ever tear Katherine to bloody shreds the way savage grizzly bears eventually would. . . .' "

ACT II, SCENE FOUR

In voice-over, we hear **Terrence Terry** reading from the revised final chapter of *Love Slave*. As we dissolve from the theater of the previous scene, we continue to hear the ambient sounds of the rehearsal: carpenters hammering scenery together, tap dancing, machine-gun fire, the dying screams of sailors burned alive, and **Lillian Hellman**. However, these noises fade as once more we see the soft-focus interior of Miss Kathie's boudoir. We see **Webster Carlton Westward III**, shot from the waist up, his naked torso shining with sweat, as he lifts one hand to his nose, the fingers dripping wet, and inhales deeply, closing his eyes. His hands drop down, out of the shot, then rise, each hand gripping a slender ankle. Lifting the two feet to shoulder height, he holds them wide apart. Webb's hips buck forward, then pull back, drive forward and pull back, while the voice-over reads, "'. . . On the final day of **Katherine Kenton**'s life, I oh-so-gently nudged

113

the prow of my aching love stick against the knotted folds of her forbidden passageway. . . .' "

Once again, the man and woman copulating are idealized versions of Webb and Miss Kathie, seen through heavy filters, their movements in slow motion, fluid, possibly even blurring.

Terry's voice continues reading, " 'The pungent aroma of her most corporeal orifice drenched my senses. My ever-mounting admiration and professional respect boiling for release, I thrust deeper into the fragile, soiled petals of her fecund rose. . . .' "

In the year preceding the **French Revolution**, according to **Terrence Terry**, the antiroyalists sought to undermine public respect for **Louis XVI** and his queen, **Marie Antoinette**, by publishing drawings which depicted the monarchs engaged in degenerate sexual behavior. These cartoons, printed in **Switzerland** and **Germany** and smuggled into **France**, accused the queen of copulating with hordes of dogs, servants, clergymen. Before the storming of the **Place de la Bastille**, before the **national razor** and **Jean-Paul Marat**, these crude line drawings infiltrated citizens' hearts as the vanguard for rebellion. Comic propaganda. Obscene little sketches and dirty stories marched as advance men, eroding respect, smoothing the path for the bloody massacre to come.

That's why the Webster specimen had written such filth.

Continuing to read from the final chapter of *Love Slave*, the voice-over of **Terrence Terry** says, " 'Plunging my steely manhood, sounding the noble depths of Katherine's succulent hindquarters, I couldn't help but experience every one of her magnificent performances. Moaning and slobbering beneath me, here was **Eleanor of Aquitaine**. Squealing and clenching, here was **Edna St. Vincent Millay**. Her diminutive waist gripped between my insatiable, beastly paws, **Zelda Fitzgerald** tossed her head, howling with every breath. . . .' "

In soft focus, the younger, idealized lovers loll, tangled in gauzy sheets. The voice of Terry reads, " 'The lovely thighs which gripped my tuberous lust had trodden the boards at **Carnegie Hall**. The **London Palladium**. The luxuriant flesh which rocked below me in synchronized bliss, the delicious symphony of our mutual devouring of each other, this delicate flower grunting at the brutal onslaught of my plunging invasion, she was **Helen of Troy. Rebecca of Sunnybrook Farm. Mary Queen of Scots** . . .' "

Chirp, cluck, bark . . . **Lady Macbeth.**

Growl, bray, tweet . . . **Mary Todd Lincoln.**

" 'Abandoning the sodden glory of her puckered shelter,' " Terry continues reading, " 'I spewed my steaming tribute, gush upon jetting gush, the pearlescent globules of my adoration and profound admiration spattering Katherine's unutterably beautiful visage. . . .' "

The idealized lovers immediately vacate the bed and begin to dress. They towel off. Without speaking, Miss Kathie applies lipstick. The specimen shines his shoes, buffing them with a horsehair brush. In separate mirrors, each inspects their own teeth, checks their profile, snarls and uses a fingernail to pick a stray hair from within their respective cheeks. All of this physical business conducted in dreamy slow motion.

Terry's voice continues to read, " 'Perhaps it was Katherine's primal nature which lured her to her doom. In retrospect, she felt at ease only among a wider variety of sentient beings, and this impulse once more prompted us to venture into society with the ravenous, imprisoned residents of the **Central Park Zoo**. . . .' "

The two lovers stroll, leaving the town house, walking west toward **Fifth Avenue**. Sunlight streams down from a clear blue sky. Songbirds twitter a bright chorus, and dazzling geraniums bloom, red and pink, in window boxes. Liveried doorman tip their hats, their gold braid flashing, as Miss Kathie passes. The idealized Miss Kathie, her face smooth, her feet gliding, almost floats along the sidewalk.

" 'To Katherine,' " continues the voice-over, " 'perhaps life itself occurred as a sort of prison she felt compelled to escape. A film star must feel akin to the beasts on display in any zoo. . . .' "

In a tracking shot, we see the lovers wander down a path, wending their way into the park, past the pond filled with sea lions. Beside the colony of emperor penguins, the idealized Webster waddles, heels together, to mimic the comic seabirds. The idealized Miss Kathie laughs, revealing her brilliant teeth and arching her willowy, slender throat. Suddenly, impulsively, she dashes ahead, out of the shot.

" 'Among the last endearments Katherine offered me, she confided that I was in possession of the most gifted, skilled male equipment that had ever existed in all recorded human history, ever. . . .' "

The voice-over says, " 'Raspberries to those grouches who had branded her box-office poison . . .' "

As Miss Kathie slowly sprints along the path, her movie-star hair streaming in the air, we hear the voice of **Terrence Terry** read, " 'I bounded in pursuit of my splendid beloved, declaring my devotion in a breathless public proclamation. In that instant of greatest joy, I threw open my arms in order to capture and embrace all the women she had been, **Cinderella** and **Harriet Tubman** and **Mary Cassatt**. . . .' "

In soft-focus slow motion, the idealized Webb runs, his

arms outstretched. As he reaches Miss Kathie, she tumbles backward, falling out of the shot.

In real time, we see the flash of pointed teeth. We hear guttural roars and hear bones breaking. A scream rings out.

" 'At that instant,' " the voice-over reads, " 'my everything, my reason for living, the idol of millions, **Katherine Kenton**, loses her footing and plummets into the grizzly bear enclosure. . . .' "

Still reading from *Love Slave*, the voice of **Terrence Terry** says, " 'The end.' "

ACT II, SCENE FIVE

While my position is not that of a private detective or a body-guard, for the present time my job tasks include plundering Webb's suitcase in search of the latest revisions to *Love Slave*. Later, I must sneak the manuscript back to its hiding place between the laundered shirts and undershorts so the Webster specimen won't realize we're savvy to his ever-evolving plot.

The fantasy murder scene dissolves into the current place and time. Once more we find ourselves in the hotel ballroom crowded with elegant guests previously seen in the awards ceremony with the senator. Here is an entirely different event, wherein my Miss Kathie is being awarded an honorary degree from **Wasser College**. On the same stage used earlier, in act one, scene nine, a distinguished man wears a tuxedo, standing at a microphone. The shot begins with the same swish pan as before, gradually slowing to a crane shot moving between the tables circled by seated guests.

Used a second time, the effect will feel a touch clichéd, thus suggesting the tedium of even Miss Kathie's seemingly glamorous life. How even lofty accolades become tiresome. Again, the upstage wall is filled with a shifting montage of vast black-and-white film clips which show my Miss Kathie as **Mrs. Caesar Augustus**, as **Mrs. Napoleon Bonaparte**, as **Mrs. Alexander the Great**. All the greatest roles of her illustrious career. Even this tribute montage is identical to the montage used in the previous scene, and as the same close-ups occur, her movie-star face begins to register as something abstract, no longer a person or even a human being, becoming a sort of trademark or logo. Symbolic and mythic as the full moon.

Speaking at the microphone, the master of ceremonies says, "Although she left school in the sixth grade, **Katherine Kenton** has earned a master's degree in life. . . ." Turning his head to one side, the speaker looks off stage right, saying, "She is a full tenured professor who has taught audiences worldwide about love and perseverance and faith. . . ."

In an eye-line match, we reveal Miss Kathie and myself standing, hidden among the shadows in the stage-right wing. She stands frozen as a statue, shimmering in a beaded gown while I apply touches of powder to her neck, her décolletage, the point of her chin. At my feet, around me sit the bags and totes and vacuum bottles that all contribute to creating this moment. The hairpieces and makeup and prescription drugs.

When *Photoplay* published the six-page pictorial showing Miss Kathie's town house interior it was my hands that folded the sharp hospital corners on every bed. True, the photographs depicted Miss Kathie with an apron tied around her waist, kneeling to scrub the kitchen floor, but only after

I'd cleaned and waxed that tile. My hands create her eyes and cheekbones. I pluck and pencil her famous eyebrows. What you see is collaboration. Only when we're combined, together, do Miss Kathie and I make one extraordinary person. Her body and my vision.

"As a teacher," says the master of ceremonies, "**Katherine Kenton** has reached innumerable pupils with her lessons of patience and hard work. . . ."

Within this tedious monologue, we dissolve to flashback: a recent sunny day in the park. As in the earlier, soft-focus murder fantasy, Miss Kathie and **Webster Carlton Westward III** stroll hand in hand toward the zoo. In a medium shot, we see Miss Kathie and Webb step to the rail which surrounds a pit full of pacing grizzly bears. Miss Kathie's hands grip the metal rail so tightly the knuckles glow white, her face frozen so near the bears, only a vein, surfacing beneath the skin of her neck, pulses and squirms to betray her terror. We hear the ambient noise of children singing. We hear lions and tigers roar. Hyenas laugh. Some jungle bird or howler monkey declares its existence, screeching a maniac's gibberish. Our entire world, always doing battle against the silence and obscurity of death.

Chirp, squawk, bray . . . **George Gobel**.

Moo, meow, oink . . . **Harold Lloyd**.

Instead of soft focus, this flashback occurs in grainy, echoing cinema verité. The only light source, the afternoon sun, flares in the camera lens, washing out the scene in brief flashes. The grizzlies stagger and bellow among the sharp rocks below. From off-camera, a peacock screams and screams with the hysterical voice of a woman being stabbed to death.

On top of all these ambient animal sounds, we still faintly

hear the master of ceremonies saying, "We bestow this honorary PhD in humanities not so much in recognition of what she's learned, but in gratitude—in our most earnest gratitude—for what **Katherine Kenton** has taught us. . . ."

Surfacing in the zoo sound track, we hear a faint heartbeat. The steady *thump-thump, thump-thump* matches the jumping pulse of the vein in Miss Kathie's neck, immediately below her jawline. Even as the animal sounds and human chatter grow more faint, the heartbeat grows louder. The heart beats faster, more loud; the tendons surface in the skin of Miss Kathie's neck, betraying her inner terror. Similar veins and tendons surface, twitching and jumping in the backs of each hand clamped to the bear pit railing.

Standing beside Miss Kathie at the rail, the Webster specimen lifts one arm and drapes it around her shoulders. Her heartbeat racing. The peacock screaming. As the Webb's arm settles over her shoulders Miss Kathie releases the rail. With both her hands, she seizes the Webb's hand dangling beside her face, pulling down on the wrist and throwing Webster, judo-style, over her back. Over the railing. Into the pit.

Dissolving back to the stage wings, the present moment, we hear a grizzly bear roar and a man's faint scream. Miss Kathie stands in the dim light reflected off the speaker. The skin of her neck, smooth, not pulsing, moving only her lipstick, she says, "Have you found any new versions of the manuscript?"

On the upstage wall, she appears as **Mrs. Leonardo da Vinci**, as **Mrs. Stephen Foster**, as **Mrs. Robert Fulton**.

Any interview, actually any promotion campaign, is equivalent to a so-called "blind date" with a stranger, where you flirt and flutter your eyelashes and try very hard not to get fucked.

In truth, the degree of anyone's success depends on how often they can say the word *yes* and hear the word *no*. Those many times you're thwarted yet persevere.

By shooting this scene with the same audience and setting as the earlier one, we can imply how all awards ceremonies are merely lovely traps baited with some bright silver-plate piece of praise. Deadly traps baited with applause.

Stooping, I twist the cap off one thermos, not the one full of black coffee, or the thermos full of chilled vodka, nor the vacuum bottle rattling with **Valium** like a **Carmen Miranda** maraca. I open another thermos bottle and pinch out the thin sheaf of pages which are rolled tight and stuffed inside. Printed along the heading of each sheet, words read *Love Slave*. A third draft. I give her the pages.

My Miss Kathie squints at the typed words. Shaking her head, she says, "I can't make heads or tails out of this. Not without my glasses." And she hands the sheets back to me, saying, "You read them. I want you to tell me how I'm going to die. . . ."

And from the audience, we hear a sudden rush of thunderous applause.

ACT II, SCENE SIX

" 'On the day she painfully fried to death,' " I read in voice-over, " 'my beloved **Katherine Kenton** enjoyed a luxuriant bubble bath.' "

As with previous final-chapter sequences read aloud from *Love Slave*, we see the younger, idealized versions of Miss Kathie and the Webb, cavorting upon her bed, in a soft-focus, misty version of her boudoir. In voice-over, I continue reading as the fantasy couple leave their lovemaking and stride, slow, trancelike, long-legged into the bedroom's adjoining bathroom.

" 'As was her custom,' " reads my voice, " 'subsequent to strenuous oral contact with my romantic meat shaft, Katherine rinsed her delicate palate with a mouthful of eau de cologne and applied chips of glistening ice to her slender, traumatized throat.

" 'As I opened the taps,' " continues the voice-over, " 'filling her sunken, pink-marble tub with frothy steaming water, I added the bath oil, and dense mounds of lather billowed. As I readied these luxuriant ablutions, my dearest Katherine said, "Webster, my darling, the pints of love essence you erupt at the peak of oral passion taste more intoxicating than gorging on even the richest European chocolate." My beloved belched demurely into her fist, swallowed and said, "All women should taste your delicious emissions." ' "

The soft-focus, idealized Miss Kathie shuts her violet eyes and licks her lips.

The fantasy couple kiss, then break their embrace.

" 'Lowering her silken sensual legs with infinite care,' " I read in voice-over, " 'Katherine immersed her spattered thighs, her acclaimed pubis descending into the scalding clouds of iridescent white. The hot liquid lapped at her satiny buttocks, then splashed at her silken bustline. The misty vapors swirled, perfume filling the sultry bathroom air.' "

My own voice continues, reading, " 'It was the year every other song on the radio was **Mitzi Gaynor** singing "**On the Atchison, Topeka and the Santa Fe**," and a large **RCA** radio sat conveniently near the edge of the pink-marble bathtub, its dial tuned to play romantic ballads, and its sturdy electrical cord plugged into a convenient wall socket.' "

We get an insert shot of said radio, balanced on the tub's rim, so close that steam condenses in sweaty droplets on the radio's wooden case.

" 'In addition,' " continues my voice, " 'an attractive assortment of electric lamps, each equipped with subdued, pink-tinted bulbs, their flattering light filtered by beaded shades, these also stood around the rim of the luxurious bubble bath.' "

A slow panning shot reveals a forest of lamps, short and

tall, balanced on the wide rim of the oversize tub. A black tangle of power cords snake from the lamps to wall outlets. Many of these thick cords, almost pulsing with electric current, look frayed.

"'Sinking up to her slender neck in the fragrant foaming bubbles,'" continues the voice-over, "'Katherine released a contented moan. At that moment of our inestimable happiness, playing the lovely **Grand Waltz Brilliant** by **Frédéric Chopin**, the radio slipped from its perilous perch. Just by accident, all the various lamps also tumbled, plunging deep into the inviting waters, poaching my beloved alive like an agonized, screaming, tortured egg. . . .'"

On camera the perfumed foam boils, billowing, rising to mask the flashing, sizzling death scene. My voice reads, "'The end.'"

ACT II, SCENE SEVEN

We cut back to the auditorium of the lavish Broadway theater where a Japanese bomb explodes, blasting shrapnel into **Yul Brynner** in the role of **Dwight D. Eisenhower**. The USS *Arizona* lists starboard, threatening to capsize on **Vera-Ellen** singing the role of **Eleanor Roosevelt**. The USS *West Virginia* keels over on top of **Neville Chamberlain** and the **League of Nations**.

As the Zeros strafe **Ivor Novello**, my Miss Kathie climbs to the foremast of the battleship, menaced by antiaircraft gunfire and **Lionel Atwill**, biting the pin of a hand grenade between her teeth. With a jerk of her head Miss Kathie pulls the pin, slingshotting her arm to fling the grenade, lobbing it too wide. The cast-iron pineapple narrowly misses **Hirohito**, and instead beans **Romani Romani** in the string section of the orchestra pit.

From an audience seat, fifth row center, a voice screams,

"Oh, stop, for fuck's sake." **Lillian Hellman** stands, brandishing a rolled copy of the score, slashing the air with it as if with a riding crop. Lilly screams, "Just stop!" She screams, "You're giving aid and comfort to the enemy!"

Onstage, the entire Japanese Imperial Army grinds to a silent halt. The dead sailors strewn across the deck of the **USS *Tennessee*** stand and twist their heads to stretch their stiff necks. **Ensign Joe Taussig** brings the **USS *Nevada*** back into port while Lilly hauls herself up onto the stage apron. Her spittle flashing in the footlights, she screams, "*Fouetté en tournant* when you throw the grenade, you stupid bitch!" To demonstrate, Hellman rises to stand, trembling on the point of one toe, then kicks her raised leg to rotate herself. Kicking and turning, she screams, "And go *all the way around*, not halfway. . . ."

In the reverse angle, we see **Terrence Terry** and myself seated at the rear of the house, surrounded by an assortment of garment bags, hatboxes and unwanted infants. The house seats are otherwise empty. Terry speculates that Miss Kathie keeps botching the grenade throw intentionally. Her previous hand grenade slammed into **Barbara Bel Geddes**. The throw before that bounced off the thick skull of **Hume Cronyn**. If Webster plans to kill her at the peak of a new stage success, Terry explains, it hardly makes sense for Miss Kathie to defeat the evil **Emperor Showa**. Rave opening-night notices will only increase her danger.

Onstage, Lilly Hellman executes a perfect pas de bourée step, at the same time putting a pistol shot between the eyes of **Buddy Ebsen**.

Handing the pistol to Miss Kathie, Hellman says, "Now, you try it. . . ."

The pistol misfires, killing **Jack Elam**. Another shot

ricochets off of the USS *New Jersey* and wounds **Cyd Charisse**.

In my lap, I scribble into a notebook. My head bowed over my work. Tucked beneath the notebook I conceal the latest revision to *Love Slave*, a fourth draft of the final chapter. A scenario beyond the omnibus crash, the grizzly bear pit, the bubble-bath electrocution.

Onstage, Lilly Hellman performs a series of jetés while leveling a flamethrower on the **Flying Escalantes**.

Across an aisle from Terry, I sit writing, the notebook pages open across my lap in the dim light. The nib of my fountain pen scratching, looping, dotting lines and sentences across each page, I say that no memory is anything more than a personal choice. A very deliberate choice. When we recall someone—a parent, a spouse, a friend—as better than they perhaps were, we do so to create an ideal, something to which we, ourselves, can aspire. But when we remember someone as a drunk, a liar, a bully, we're only creating an excuse for our own poor behavior.

Still writing, I say how the same can be said for the people who read such books. The best people look for lofty role models such as the **Katherine Kenton** I've given my life to create. Other readers will seek out the tawdry strumpet depicted in **Webster Carlton Westward III**'s book, for comfort and license in their own tawdry, disordered lives.

All human beings search for either reasons to be good, or excuses to be bad.

Call me an elitist, but I'm no patch on **Mary Pickford**.

Onstage, Lilly claps her hands together twice and says, "Okay, let's take it from the point where shards of bomb casing shred **Captain Mervyn Bennion**."

In silence, everyone present, from **Ricardo Cortez** to

Hope Lange, says fervent prayers to live beyond Miss Hellman, and thus to avoid being posthumously absorbed into her hideous self-mythology. Her name-dropping **Tourette's syndrome**, set to music by **Otto Harbach**. In the presence of Miss Hellman, there are no atheists.

Lilly Hellman screams, "Katherine!"

Miss Kathie screams, "Hazie!"

Hiss, bray, bark . . . **Jesus Christ.**

We all have some proper noun to blame.

The truth about Miss Kathie's poor performance is that she's always looking for the stray mortar shell or rifle round intended to end her life. She can't concentrate for fear she's missed reading any new draft of *Love Slave* and might be killed at any moment. An exploding battleship. A stage light plummeting from the flies. Any prop collapsible stage knife might be replaced with an actual dagger, wielded by some unknowing Japanese soldier or **Allan Dwan**. As we sit here, **Webster Carlton Westward III** could be planting a bomb or pumping poison gas into Miss Kathie's backstage dressing room. Under such circumstances, of course she can't manage an adequate pas de deux.

Terry says, "Why do you stay with her?" He asks me, "Why have you stayed with her for all these years?"

Because, I say, the life of **Katherine Kenton** is my work-in-progress. **Mrs. Lord Byron, Mrs. Pope Innocent VI** and **Mrs. Kaiser von Hindenburg** might be Miss Kathie's best work, but she is mine. Still writing, still scribbling away, I say that Miss Katie is my unfinished masterpiece, and an artist does not abandon the work when it becomes difficult. Or when the artwork chooses to become involved with inappropriate men. My job title is not that of nanny or guardian angel, but I perform duties of both. My full-time profession is what **Walter Winchell** calls a "star sitter." A "celebrity curator," according to **Elsa Maxwell**.

I retrieve the most recent draft of Webster's torrid tell-all and offer it across the aisle to Terry.

From his seat, Terry asks, "How come she's not electrocuted?"

Miss Kathie hasn't taken a bath in days, I tell him.

She reeks of what **Louella Parsons** would call "aroma *d'amore*."

Terry reaches across, taking the pages from my outstretched hand. Scanning the top sheet, he reads, " 'No one could've anticipated that by the end of this day my most beloved Katherine would shatter every single, solitary bone in her alluring body, and her glamorous Hollywood blood would be spattered over half of Midtown Manhattan . . .' "

ACT II, SCENE EIGHT

The voice of **Terrence Terry** continues as an audio bridge from the previous scene, reading, "'... my most beloved Katherine would shatter every single, solitary bone in her alluring body, and her glamorous Hollywood blood would be spattered over half of Midtown Manhattan ...'" as we dissolve once more into a fantasy sequence. Here, the lithe, idealized Webster and Miss Kathie cavort about the open-air observation deck on the eighty-sixth floor of the **Empire State Building**.

In voice-over Terry reads, "'In celebration of the six-month anniversary of our first introduction, I'd rented the loftiest aerie on the fabled isle of Manahatta.'" He reads aloud, "'There, I'd staged a romantic dinner for two catered from three thousand miles away by **Perino's**.'"

The mise-en-scène includes a table set for two, draped with a white cloth, and crowded with crystal stemware, silver and china. **Julian Eltinge** tinkles the ivories of a grand piano which has been winched up for the evening. **Judy Holliday** sings a program of **Marc Blitzstein** and **Marc Connelly** songs, backed by the **Royal Ballet Sinfonia** and **Myrna Loy**. In every direction, the spires of **New York City** blaze with lights.

The voice of **Terrence Terry** reads, " 'Only the crème de la crème of waiters and entertainers were present, all of them snugly blindfolded as in the **Erich von Stroheim** masterpiece *The Wedding March*, so Katherine and I would not feel self-conscious as we indulged our carnal assaults upon each other.' "

To highlight the fact that this constitutes their umpteenth sex scene, the willowy, soft-focus Miss Kathie and Webster copulate perfunctorily, as if robots, not looking at one another. With their eyes rolled back within their heads, their tongues hanging out the corners of their mouths, panting like beasts, the pair change position without speaking, the wet slap of their colliding genitals threatening to drown out the live music.

" 'We made love beneath a billion stars and above a sea of ten million electric lights. There, between heaven and earth, blindfolded waiters tipped bottles of **Moët champagne** directly into our greedy, guzzling mouths, splashing bubbly upon Katherine's savory bosoms, even as I continued to pleasure her insatiable loins and oblivious waiters slid a succession of chilled, raw oysters down the slippery chute of her regal throat. . . . ' "

The fornicating pair continue to couple. **Jimmy Durante** steps up to the microphone, blindfolded, and sings "**Sentimental Journey**."

" 'In keeping with my planned tribute,' " reads the

voice-over of **Terrence Terry**, " 'at the instant of Katherine's bucking, clenching *petite mort*, various steaming rivulets of her feminine juices cascading down each of her sculpted thighs, upon that crescendo of passion, the assortment of floodlights which bathe the apex of the tower were activated by an unseen hand. The searing light which broke upon us, rather than being the usual white hue, shone tonight in the exact same shade as Katherine's insanely violet eyes. . . .' "

The pair step apart and begin absently wiping at their sopping groins, using dinner napkins they then wad and drop. Similarly soiled linen napkins litter the rooftop as the pair continue mopping themselves with the hanging hem of the white tablecloth.

" 'Within moments,' " reads Terry, " 'we'd severed our fleshy bond and sat dressed impeccably in evening finery, enjoying an elegant flavorful repast of roasted squab served on **Limoges** china alongside cooked carrots and garlic, double-stuffed baked potatoes or the option of a small dinner salad with ranch dressing or rice pilaf.

" ' "Webster," said Katherine, "you stupendously virile male animal, this majestic tower is your only phallic rival in the world." Adding with a lascivious grin, "And I'd gladly climb a million steps to sit atop both. . . ." ' "

In contrast with the ripe voice-over, the dreamy, idealized Miss Kathie and Webster merely devour the food quickly, swilling wine, their cutlery clattering against their plates, swallowing so quickly their belches threaten to overwhelm the singing. With greasy fingers they gnaw the tiny squab carcasses, spitting the chewed bones from their mouths toward the street far below. The blindfolded waiters stagger about.

Despite such louche behavior, the voice of **Terrence Terry** continues reading, oblivious, " 'Even now as Katherine and I stood and strode to the tower's lofty parapet, preparing to raise our glasses in a champagne toast to this, the world's most glamorous city, countless lesser mortals dwelt at our feet, unaware of the bliss which existed so far above their heads. Somewhere below wandered **Elia Kazan**, **Arthur Treacher** and **Anne Baxter**, each in their own limited existence. Down there drifted **William Koenig**, **Rudy Vallee**, and **Gracie Allen**, no doubt imagining they lived lives of rich fulfillment. But no, if **Mary Miles Minter**, **Leslie Howard** and **Billy Bitzer** were indeed so wise and aware then they would've been us.' "

The idealized man and woman shove themselves away from the dinner table, grab their drinks and lurch to the building's edge.

" 'In hindsight,' " says the voice-over, " 'perhaps we too were blinded by our supreme happiness. "Oh, Katherine," I distinctly recall saying, "I do so love, love, *love* you!" Communicating this sentiment not merely with my probing love pipe, but also my mouth. If I dare say it—with my very life's breath, every word comingled with the lingering aftertaste of her saucy nethers. . . .' "

The star-filtered, stylized version of Miss Kathie tosses back the last of her champagne and hands the empty glass to the idealized Webster. Even as the blindfolded musicians continue to saw away on their violins, the Webster substitute checks his wristwatch and yawns, patting his open mouth with the palm of one hand.

" 'During that blazing violet moment of our splendorous adoration,' " reads the voice-over, " 'Katherine's elegantly shod foot skidded against a leftover layer of our spent passion. In that infamous moment, mankind's most dazzling star fell, a flashing, shrieking **Halley's Comet** hurtling to the bustling sidewalks of **West Thirty-fourth Street.**'"

The Katherine stand-in shrugs her perfect shoulders in resignation. She kicks off both her high-heeled shoes, climbs the guardrail and swan-dives into the abyss. The idealized Webster stand-in watches her plunge; then he stoops to collect her discarded high heels and flings them after her.

Terry's voice reads, "'The end.'"

ACT II, SCENE NINE

Forgive me, please, but I must violate the fourth wall once more. Even as Miss Kathie dodges and parries the attempts on her life, a curious reversal appears to be taking place. The constant threat of violent death sculpts **Katherine Kenton** down to tensed muscle. The perennial threat of poisoning deadens her appetite, and the need to be continually vigilant deters her from indulging in pills and alcohol. Under such strain, her spine has stiffened with resolve. Her carriage stands erect, her stomach is hollowed, and she carries herself with the bravado of a soldier advancing onto a field of battle. The presence of death, always haunting, always at hand, has awakened a sense of vibrant life within her. Roses bloom in the cheeks of my Miss Kathie. Her violet eyes sparkle, alert for sudden danger.

More than all the plastic surgeries and all the cosmetics

in existence, the terror of her imminent destruction has brought Miss Kathie back to glowing, youthful life.

In contrast, **Webster Carlton Westward III**, once so young and ideal, now appears haggard, wounded, battle-scarred, his handsome face strafed with wrinkles . . . scratches . . . stitches. The Webb specimen's dense hair sheds itself in daily strands and clumps. Thwarted at each turn, he adopts the whipped demeanor of a cowering dog.

Still he perseveres, whatever his motives, to endear himself with my Miss Kathie. Always there's the chance of an assassination plot we haven't previewed, and Miss Kathie must forever be on guard. Once, in her heightened wariness, she pushed young Webster down a flight of stairs near the **Bethesda Fountain**, and he still staggers with a limp, a steel pin surgically embedded to heal his shattered ankle. On another occasion, at **the Russian Tea Room** when she misjudged a quick movement of his as possibly malevolent, she lanced his arm with a steak knife in preemptive self-defense. Another time, she pushed him from a subway platform. His all-American face looks livid and swollen from the burns caused when Miss Kathie assaulted him with a flaming **bananas Foster**. His bright brown eyes are dull and bloodshot from a prophylactic blast of Miss Kathie's mace.

Thus the reversal: as Miss Kathie becomes more vital and vibrant, the Webster specimen falls into increasing decrepitude. A stranger, meeting the pair for the first time, would be hard-pressed to name the younger and the older. With her haughty expression, it's difficult to decide which Miss Kathie finds more disgusting: Webster's apparent plots to murder her, or his declining physical virility.

And with every scar and burn and scratch, this defaced

Webster specimen looks more like the monster I warned Miss Kathie against.

In a hard transition, we cut back to final dress rehearsal for the new **Broadway** show, at the moment the music is peaking with the voices of the entire cast singing, while Miss Kathie raises the American flag on **Iwo Jima**, assisted by **Jack Webb** and **Akim Tamiroff**. A **Florenz Ziegfeld** chorus line of **Mack Sennett** beauties gotten up as imperial Japanese airmen in low-cut, peekaboo costumes by **Edith Head** link arms and execute precision high kicks which expose their fascist buttocks. The spectacle fills a medium shot, busy with motion, color and music, until the shot pulls back to reveal the audience seats are—once more—almost all vacant.

Luise Rainer sings slightly off-key during the **Rape of Nanking**, and **Conrad Veidt** flubbed a couple dance steps during the **Corregidor Death March**, but otherwise the first act seems to work. A constant plume, really a mushroom cloud of white cigarette smoke rises from Lilly Hellman's seat in the center of the fifth row, flanked there by **Michael Curtiz** and **Sinclair Lewis**. On **West Forty-seventh Street** already the marquee carries the title *Unconditional Surrender* starring **Katherine Kenton** and **George Zucco**. Music and lyrics by **Jerome Kern** and **Woody Guthrie**. At the stage door, a truck from the printer unloads stacks of glossy programs. Backstage, **Eli Wallach** in the role of **Howard Hughes** practices some business, seated within the cockpit of a full-size balsa-wood mock-up of the *Spruce Goose*.

The first act curtain falls as the chorus girls rush to change into their sequined shark costumes for the sinking of the USS *Indianapolis* at the opening of the second act. **Ray Bolger**

prepares to die of congestive heart failure as **Franklin Delano Roosevelt**. **John Mack Brown** preps to assume office as **Harry Truman** opposite a small cameo appearance by **Ann Southern** as **Margaret Truman**.

Amid the sea of empty seats, **Terrence Terry** and I sit in the twentieth row center, buttressed by our parcels and **Bloomingdale's** bags and various **thermos** bottles.

Alone in row twelve, stage right, sits **Webster Carlton Westward III**, his bright brown eyes never leaving the form of Miss Kathie. His broad shoulders leaning forward, both his elbows planted on his knees, he thrusts his American face toward her light.

From any closer than row fifteen, Miss Kathie's dyed hair looks stiff as wire. Her gestures, jittery and tense, her body whittled down by fear and anxiety to what **Louella Parsons** would call a "lipsticked stick figure." Despite the constant threat of murder, she refuses to involve the police out of fear she'll be humiliated by **W. H.** **Mooring** in *Film Weekly* or **Hale Horton** in *Photoplay*, depicted as a dotty has-been infatuated by a scheming gigolo. It's a choice between **the devil** and the deep blue sea: whether to be killed and humiliated in book form by the Webb, or to remain alive and be humiliated by **Donovan Pedelty** or **Miriam Gibson** in *Screen Book* magazine.

Even as the stagehands change the plaster rocks of **Iwo Jima** for the canvas hull of the doomed *Indianapolis*, I'm scribbling notes. My fountain pen scratching my hand-writing along line after line, I scheme and conspire to save my Miss Kathie.

Eyeing the Webster specimen, the matinee idol outline of Webb's American profile, Terry asks if we've discovered any new murder plan.

Midsentence, still writing, I retrieve the latest pages of *Love Slave* and toss them into Terry's lap. I tell him that I found this newest revision in Webster's suitcase this morning.

Terry asks if I've arranged an escort for the show's opening next week. If not, he can stop by the town house to collect me. His eyes skimming back and forth across the typed pages, Terry asks if Miss Kathie has seen this version of her demise.

Flipping to a new page of my notebook, still writing, I tell him, Yes. That accounts for her vibrato.

Peering over the top of the *Love Slave* pages, squinting at my notes, he asks what I'm writing.

Tax returns, I tell him. I shrug and say that I'm answering Miss Kathie's fan mail. Reviewing her contracts and investments. Nothing special. Nothing too important.

And reading aloud from the new finale of Miss Kathie's life story, Terry says, " '**Katherine Kenton** never knew it, but the Japanese Yakuza are deservedly world-renowned as ruthless, bloodthirsty assassins. . . .' "

ACT II, SCENE TEN

"'A Yakuza assassin,'" reads the voice of **Terrence Terry**, "'can perform an execution in as little as three seconds. . . .'" We dissolve to a misty street scene. The fantasy stand-ins for Miss Kathie and Webster stroll, window-shopping along a deserted city sidewalk, gilded by a rind of magic-hour sunlight. Whether this is dawn or dusk, one can't tell for certain. The lithesome pair linger at display windows, Miss Kathie perusing dazzling necklaces and bracelets proffered there, dense and heavily set with glittering clusters of diamonds and rubies, even as Webster never takes his eyes off her face, as bewitched by her beauty as she is by the resplendent wealth of lavish, sparkling stones.

The voice-over continues reading, "'A common assassination technique is to approach the target from behind. . . .'"

Trailing a few steps in the wake of Miss Kathie, we see

a figure dressed in all-black garments, his face concealed within a black ski mask. Black gloves cover his hands.

"'What actually occurred may always be one of filmland's most enduring mysteries. No one could say who had paid for the gruesome attack,'" says Terry's voice, "'but it did exhibit all the earmarks of a professionally trained killer. . . .'"

The happy couple saunter along, aware of only the glittering gems and their own happiness. They move in the slow-motion bubble of their own supreme bliss.

"'The weapon was an ordinary ice pick . . .'" reads Terry.

We see the masked figure extricate a gleaming spike of needle-sharp steel from his jacket pocket.

"'The assailant has merely to step close to the victim's back . . .'" reads Terry in voice-over.

The masked figure sidles up immediately behind Miss Kathie. Shadowing her footsteps, he reaches toward her svelte neck with the cruelly sharpened ice pick.

"'Thereupon, the well-practiced assassin extends an arm over the victim's shoulder and plunges the steely weapon's point deep into the soft area above the clavicle,'" reads Terry. "'A quick side-to-side jerk effectively severs the subclavian artery and phrenic nerve, causing fatal exsanguination and suffocation within an instant. . . .'"

Yeah, yeah, yeah, on-screen all this happens. Blood and gore spray an adjacent shopwindow filled with sparkling, glistening diamonds and sapphires. The clots and gobbets of gore slide streaks of brilliant crimson down the polished glass even as the masked assailant flees, his running footfalls echoing down **Fifth Avenue**. At the death scene, **Webster Carlton Westward III** kneels in the spreading pool of Miss Kathie's scarlet blood, cradling her movie-star face in his massive, masculine hands. The light in her famous violet eyes fading, fading, fading.

" 'With her final dying breath,' " reads **Terrence Terry**, " 'my beloved Katherine said, "Webb, please promise me . . ." She said, "Honor and remember me by sharing your incredibly talented penis with all the most beautiful but less fortunate women of this world." ' "

On-screen, the idealized Miss Kathie sags, limp, in the embrace of the soft-focus Webster. Tears stream down his face as his stand-in says, "I swear." Shaking one bloody fist at the sky in frustrated rage, he shouts, "Oh, my dearest Katherine, I swear to perform your dying wish to my utmost."

From behind their thin scrim of red gore, the diamonds and sapphires watch, glinting coldly. Their multitude of polished, flashing facets reflect infinite versions of Miss Kathie's demise and Webster's unbearable heartbreak. The emeralds and rubies bear detached, timeless, eternal witness to the drama and folly of mere humankind. The Webster character looks down; seeing blood on his **Rolex** wristwatch, he hurriedly wipes the timepiece on Miss Kathie's dress, then presses the dial to his ear to listen for a tick.

Reading from the *Love Slave* manuscript, Terry says, " 'The end.' "

ACT II, SCENE ELEVEN

Professional gossip **Elsa Maxwell** once said, "All biographies are an assemblage of untruths." A beat later, adding, "So are all *autobiographies*."

The critics were willing to forgive **Lillian Hellman** a few factual inaccuracies concerning the **Second World War**. As presented here, this was history—but better. It might not be the actual war, but this was the war we wished we'd fought. For that, it was brilliant, dense and meaty, with **Maria Montez** slitting the throat of **Lou Costello**. After that, **Bob Hope** tap-dancing his signature shim-sham step through a field of live land mines.

Compared to the opening night of *Unconditional Surrender*, no doughboy crouched in the trenches nor GI in a tank turret ever shook with as much fear as my Miss Kathie felt stepping out on that stage. She made a ready target from every seat in the house. Dancing and singing, she was a

sitting duck. Each note or kick step could easily be her last, and who would notice amidst the barrage of fake bullets and mortar shells that rocked the theater that night? Any wily assassin could squeeze off a fatal shot and make his escape while the theatergoers applauded Miss Kathie's bursting skull or chest, thinking the death blow was merely a very effective special effect. Mistaking her spectacular public murder for simply a plot point in Lilly Hellman's epic saga.

So Miss Kathie danced. She occupied every inch of the set as if her life depended on it, constantly dodging and evading any single location on the stage, climbing to the forecastle of a battleship, then diving into the warm waves of the **Pacific Ocean**, the lyric of an **Arthur Freed** song bubbling up through the water, and Miss Kathie breaking the azure surface a moment later, still holding the same **Harold Arlen** note.

It was terror that invested her performance with such energy, such verve, spurring the best Miss Kathie had given her audience in decades. Creating an evening which people would recall for the remainder of their lives. Imbuing Miss Kathie with a kinetic vitality which had been too long absent. Peppered throughout the audience we see **Senator Phelps Russell Warner** seated beside his latest wife. We see **Paco Esposito** in the company of industry sexpot **Anita Page**. Myself, I sit with **Terrence Terry**. In fact, the only empty seat in the house is beside the haggard **Webster Carlton Westward III**, where he's lovingly placed the massive armload of red roses he, no doubt, intends to present during the curtain calls. A bouquet large enough to conceal a tommy gun or rifle. The barrel perhaps equipped with a silencer, although such a precaution would be wholly unnecessary as deafening Japanese Zeros dive-bomb the American forces at **Pearl Harbor**.

Tonight's performance amounted to nothing less than a battle for her identity. This, the constant creation of herself. This strutting and bellowing, a struggle to keep herself in the world, to not be replaced by another's version, the way food is digested, the way a tree's dead carcass becomes fuel or furniture. In her high stepping, Miss Kathie endlessly blared proof of her human existence. In her blurred **Bombershay** steps here was a fragile organism doing its most to effect the environment surrounding it and postponing decomposition as long as possible.

Framed in that spotlight, we watched an infant shrieking for a breast to suckle. There was a zebra or rabbit screaming as wolves tore it to pieces.

This wasn't any mere song and dance; here was a bold, blaring declaration howling itself into the empty face of death.

Before us strutted something more than Miss Kathie's past characters: **Mrs. Gunga Din** or **Mrs. Hunchback of Notre Dame** or **Mrs. Last of the Mohicans**.

No one except myself and **Terrence Terry** would take note of the sweat drenching my Miss Kathie. Or notice the twitching, nervous way her eyes rattled in their attempt to watch every seat in the orchestra and balcony. For once, the critics weren't her worst fear, not **Frank S. Nugent** of the *New York Times* nor **Howard Barnes** of the *New York Herald Tribune* nor **Robert Garland** of the *New York American*.

Jack Grant of *Screen Book*, **Gladys Hall** and **Katherine Albert** of *Modern Screen* magazine, **Harrison Carroll** of the *Los Angeles Herald Express*, a legion of critics take rapturous notes, racking their brains for additional superlatives. Also, columnists **Sheilah Graham** and **Earl Wilson**, a group that any other show, any other night would constitute what **Dor-**

othy Kilgallen calls "a jury of her sneers," this night those sourpusses would clamor with praise.

In my seat, I jot my own notes, making a record of this triumph. Tonight, not only Miss Kathie's triumph and Lilly Hellman's, but my own personal victory; the sensation feels as if I've seen my own crippled child begin to walk.

At my elbow, Terry whispers that producer **Dick Castle** telephoned, already angling for the film rights. Looking pointedly at my feet tapping along to the music, he smiles and whispers, "Who died and made you **Eleanor Powell**?" His own tense hands carry a constant stream of colorful **Jordan almonds** from a small paper sack to his mouth.

Onstage, my Miss Kathie belts out another surefire gold-record hit, wrapping herself in the smoldering, snapping flag of the **USS *Arizona***. Throwing herself from stage left to stage right she displays the panicked, manic struggle of an animal caught in a trap. Or a butterfly snared in a spider's web. Spangles flashing, vivid eye shadow, her hair colored and sculpted beyond the lurid dreams of any peacock, the smile she displays is nothing more than a jaws-open, teeth-snarling rictus spasming in outrage against the dying light. Bug-eyed in her forced enthusiasm, Miss Kathie thrashes through each production number, a frenzied, vicious, frenetic denial of impending death.

Her every gesture wards away an unseen attacker, keeping the invisible at bay. Her every freeze, drop, drag and slide constitutes a fight, sidestep, evasion of her imminent doom. Pounding the boards, my Miss Kathie spins as a flapping, squawking, frantic dervish begging for another hour of life. So upbeat, so animated and alive in this moment because death looms so close.

Backstage, desperate for an encore he knows the audience

will demand, **Dore Schary** already plans to A-bomb **Nagasaki**. For a second and third encore, he's chosen **Tokyo** and **Yokohama**.

According to **Walter Winchell**, the entire **Second World War** was just an encore to the first.

Onstage, Miss Kathie executes a violent, furious **Buffalo** step, transitioning to a **Suzy Q** even as **Manchuria** falls. **Hong Kong** and **Malaysia** topple. **Mickey Rooney** as **Ho Chi Minh** leads the **Viet Minh** into battle. The **Doolittle Raid** rains fire on **Nora Bayes**.

And in the seat next to me, **Terrence Terry** clutches at his throat with both hands and slides, lifeless, to the floor.

ACT III, SCENE ONE

For this next scene, we open with a booming, thundering chord from a pipe organ. The chord continues, joining the melody of **Felix Mendelssohn**'s Wedding March. As the scene takes shape, we see my Miss Kathie garbed in a wedding gown, standing in a small room dominated by a large stained-glass window. Beyond an open doorway, we can make out the arched, cavernous interior of a cathedral where row upon row of people line the pews.

A small constellation of stylists orbit Miss Kathie. **Sydney Guilaroff** and **M. La Barbe** tuck away stray hairs, patting and smoothing the sides of Miss Kathie's pristine updo. **Max Factor** dabs the finishing touches on her makeup. My position is not that of a bridesmaid or flower girl. I am not a formal member of the wedding party, but I shake out Miss Kathie's train and spread its full length. At the back of the church I tell her to smile, and slip my finger between her lips to scratch a smear of lipstick off one upper incisor. I toss the veil over her head and ask if she's certain she wants to do this.

Her violet eyes gleaming behind the haze of Belgian lace, vivid as flowers under a layer of hoarfrost, Miss Kathie says, "*C'est la vie.*"

She says, "That's Russian talk for 'I do.'"

In an impulsive gesture I lift her veil and lean forward, putting my lips to her powdered cheek. There, the taste of **Mitsouko** perfume and the dust of talc meet my mouth. Ducking my head and twisting my face away, I sneeze.

My darling Miss Kathie says, "*Ich liebe dich.*" Adding, "That's how the French say, 'Gesundheit.'"

Standing near us, donning a dove gray morning coat, **Lillian Hellman** snaps her fingers—one snap, two snaps, three snaps—and jerks her head toward the pews filled with guests. Lilly offers her arm and links it through Miss Kathie's, guiding her to the head of the church's center aisle. My Miss Kathie's arms, garbed in white, elbow-length gloves, her gloved hands clasp a bouquet of white roses, freesia and snowdrops. **The Vienna Boys Choir** sings "**Some Enchanted Evening.**" **Marian Anderson** sings "**I'm Just a Girl Who Can't Say No.**" The **Sammy Kaye Orchestra** plays "**Greensleeves**" as the shining satin and white lace of Miss Kathie drifts a step, drifts a step, drifts another step away, leaving me. Arm in arm with Lilly, she stalks closer to the altar, where **Fanny Brice** stands as the matron of honor. **Louis B. Mayer** waits to officiate. A bower arches above them, twining with countless pink **Nancy Reagan** roses and yellow lilies. Among the flowers loom a thicket of newsreel cameras and boom microphones.

Miss Kathie walks what **Walter Winchell** calls "the bridal mile" wearing what **Sheilah Graham** calls "very off-white" posing what **Hedda Hopper** calls a "veiled threat."

"Something old, something new, something borrowed," **Louella Parsons** would write in her column, "and something extremely fishy."

Miss Kathie seems too ready to be placed under what **Elsa Maxwell** calls "spouse arrest."

At the altar **Lon McCallister** cools his heels as best man, standing next to a brown pair of eyes. This year's groom, the harried, haggard, battle-scarred **Webster Carlton Westward III**.

Crowding the bride's side of the church, the guests include **Kay Francis** and **Donald O'Connor**, **Deanna Durbin** and **Mildred Coles**, **George Bancroft** and **Bonita Granville** and **Alfred Hitchcock**, **Franchot Tone** and **Greta Garbo**, all the people who failed to attend the funeral for little **Loverboy**.

As **Metro-Goldwyn-Mayer** would say, "More stars than there are in heaven . . ."

On her trip to the altar, my Miss Kathie throws looks and kisses to **Cary Grant** and **Theda Bara**. She waves a white-gloved hand at **Arthur Miller** and **Deborah Kerr** and **Danny Kaye**. From behind her veil she smiles at **Johnny Walker**, **Laurence Olivier**, **Randolph Scott** and **Freddie Bartholomew**, **Buddy Pepper**, **Billy Halop**, **Jackie Cooper** and a tiny **Sandra Dee**.

Her gaze wafting to a familiar mustache, Miss Kathie sighs, "**Groucho!**"

It's through a veil that my darling Miss Kathie most looks like her true self. Like someone who throws you a look from the window of a train, or from the opposite side of a busy street, blurred behind speeding traffic, a face whom you could wed in that moment and imagine yourself happy to live with forever. Her face, balanced and composed, so full of potential and possibility, she looks like the answer to everything wrong. Just to meet her violet eyes feels like a blessing.

In the basement of this same building, within the crypt that holds her former "was-band" **Oliver "Red" Drake, Esq.**, alongside the ashes of **Lothario** and **Romeo** and **Loverboy**, amid the dead soldiers of empty champagne bottles, down there waits the mirror which contains her every secret. That defaced mirror of **Dorian Gray**, it forms a death mask even as the world kills her a little more each year. That scratched web of scars etched by myself wielding the same **Harry Winston** diamond that the Webster specimen now slips on her finger.

But wrapped in the lace of a wedding veil my Miss Kathie always becomes a promising new future. The camera lights flare amidst the flowers, the heat wilting and scorching the roses and lilies. The smell of sweet smoke.

This wedding scene reveals Webb as a brilliant actor, taking Miss Kathie in his arms he bends her backward, helpless, as his lips push her even further off balance. His bright brown eyes sparkle. His gleaming smile simply moons and beams.

Miss Kathie hurtles her bouquet at a crowd that includes **Lucille Ball, Janet Gaynor, Cora Witherspoon** and **Marjorie Main** and **Marie Dressler**. A mad scramble ensues between **June Allyson, Joan Fontaine** and **Margaret O'Brien**. Out of the fray **Ann Rutherford** emerges clutching the flowers. We all throw rice supplied by **Ciro's**.

Zasu Pitts cuts the wedding cake. **Mae Murray** minds the guest book.

In a quiet moment during which Miss Kathie has exited

to change out of her wedding gown, I sidle up beside the groom. As my wedding gift to Webb, I slip him a few sheets of printed paper.

Those dulled brown eyes look at the pages, reading the words *Love Slave* typed across the top margin, and he says, "What's this?"

Brushing rice from the shoulders of his coat, I say, "Don't play coy. . . ."

Those pages already belong to him, stolen from his suitcase, I'm merely returning them to their rightful owner. Saying this, I straighten his boutonniere, smoothing his lapels.

Lifting the first page, scanning it, the Webb reads, " 'No one will ever know why **Katherine Kenton** committed suicide on what seemed like such a joyous occasion. . . .' " His bright brown eyes look at me, then back to the page, and he continues to read.

ACT III, SCENE TWO

We continue with the audio bridge of **Webster Carlton Westward III** reading, " '. . . **Katherine Kenton** committed suicide on what seemed like such a joyous occasion.' "

The mise-en-scène shows my Miss Kathie in her dressing room, backstage, the soft-focus stand-in perfect and lovely as if filmed through a veil. We watch as she sits at her dressing table, leaning into her reflection in the mirror, fixing the final smears of blood and scars and crusted scabs for her upcoming **Guadalcanal** battle scene. From outside the closed dressing room door we hear a voice call, "Two minutes, Miss Kenton."

The voice-over continues reading, " 'It had long been rumored that **Oliver "Red" Drake, Esq.**, had taken his own life, after traces of cyanide were uncovered following his sudden death. Although no suicide note was ever found, and a subsequent inquest was unable to reach a conclusion, Drake

was reported to be severely despondent, according to Katherine's maid, **Hazie Coogan**. . . .'"

On Miss Kathie's dressing table, among the jars of greasepaint and hairbrushes, we see a small paper bag; the sides are rolled down to reveal its contents as a colorful array of **Jordan almonds**. Miss Kathie's lithe movie-star hand carries the almonds, a red one, a green one, a white one, almond by almond, to her mouth. At the same time, her violet eyes never leave her own reflection in the mirror. A glass bottle, prominently labeled CYANIDE, sits next to the candied almonds. The bottle's stopper removed.

Webb's voice-over continues, "'It's likely that my adored Katherine feared losing the happiness she'd struggled so long and hard to attain.'"

We see the idealized, slender version of Miss Kathie stand and adjust her military costume, studying her reflection in the dressing room mirror.

The voice of Webster reads, "'After so many years, my beloved Katherine had regained her stardom in the lead of a **Broadway** hit. She'd triumphed over a decade of drug abuse and eating disorders. And most important, she'd found a sexual satisfaction beyond anything she'd ever dreamed possible.'"

The **Katherine Kenton** fantasy stand-in lifts a tube of lipstick, twists it to its full red length and reaches toward the mirror. Over the beautiful reflection of herself, she writes: *Webster's amazing, massive penis is the only joy in this world that I will miss.* She writes, *As the French would say . . . Adios.* The fantasy version of Miss Kathie dashes a tear from her eye, turning quickly and exiting the dressing room.

As the shot follows her, Miss Kathie dashes through the maze of backstage props, unused sets and loitering stagehands;

the voice-over reads, "'According to the statements of Miss Hazie, **Oliver "Red" Drake, Esq.**, had often talked in private about ending his own life. Despite the general public impression that he and Katherine were deeply, devotedly in love, Miss Hazie testified that a morose, secret depression had settled over him. Perhaps it was this same secret sorrow which now drove my exquisite Katherine to eat those tainted sweets only minutes before the hit show's finale.'"

Onstage, Japanese bombs pelt the ships of **Pearl Harbor**. Under this pounding cascade of exploding death, the svelte Miss Kathie leaps from stage right, bounding up the tilting deck of the **USS** *Arizona*. Already, her complexion has paled, turned pallid beneath the surface of her pancake makeup.

In voice-over, we hear Webster reading, "'At the greatest moment of the greatest career of the greatest actress who has ever lived, the rainbow reds and greens and whites of those fatal candies still tingeing her luscious lips . . .'"

At the highest point of the doomed battleship, the ideal Miss Kathie stands at attention and salutes her audience.

"'At that moment, in what was clearly and undeniably a romantic self-murder,'" the voice-over continues, "'my dearest Katherine, the greatest love of my life, blew a kiss to me, where I sat in the sixth row . . . and she succumbed.'"

Still saluting, the figure collapses, plunging into the azure tropical water.

The voice of Webster reads, "'The end.'"

ACT III, SCENE THREE

We open with the distinct pop of a champagne cork, dissolving to reveal Miss Kathie and myself standing in the family crypt. Froth spills from the bottle she holds, splashing on the stone floor as Miss Kathie hurries to pour wine into the two dusty champagne glasses I hold. Here, in the depths of stone beneath the cathedral where she was so recently wed, Miss Kathie takes a glass and lifts it, toasting a new urn which rests on the stone shelf beside the urns engraved *Oliver "Red" Drake, Esq.*, *Loverboy*, *Lothario*. All of her long-dead loved ones.

The new urn of shining, polished silver sits engraved with the name **Terrence Terry**, and includes a smudged lipstick kiss identical to the old kisses dried to the magenta of ancient blood, almost black on the urns now rusted and tarnished with age.

Miss Kathie lifts her glass in a toast to this newest silver urn, saying, "*Bonne nuit*, Terrence." She sips the champagne, adding, "That's Spanish for bon voyage."

Around us a few flickering candles light the dusty, cold crypt, shimmering amid the clutter of empty wine bottles. Dirty champagne glasses hold dead spiders, each spider curled like a bony fist. Abandoned ashtrays hold stubbed cigarettes smudged with a long history of lipstick shades, the cigarettes yellowed, the lipstick faded from red to pink. Ashes and dust. The mirror of Miss Kathie's real face, scratched and scarred with her past, lies facedown among the souvenirs and sacrifices of everything she's left behind. The pill bottles half-full of **Tuinal** and **Dexamyl**. **Nembutal**, **Seconal** and **Demerol**.

Tossing back her champagne and pouring herself another glass, Miss Kathie says, "I think we ought to record this occasion, don't you?"

She means for me to prop the mirror in its upright position while she stands on the lipstick X marked on the floor. Miss Kathie holds out her left hand to me, her fingers spread so I can remove her **Harry Winston** diamond solitaire. When her face aligns with the mirror, her eyes perfectly bracketed by the crow's-feet, her lips centered between the scratched hollows and sagging cheeks, only when she's exactly superimposed on the record of her past . . . do I take the diamond and begin to draw.

On the opening night of *Unconditional Surrender*, she says Terry had paid her a visit backstage, in her dressing room before the first curtain. In the chaos of telegrams and flowers, it's likely Terry purloined the **Jordan almonds**. He'd stopped to convey his best wishes and inadvertently made off with the poisoned candy, saving her life. Poor Terrence. The accidental martyr.

As Miss Kathie speculates, I plow the diamond along the soft surface of the mirror, gouging her new wrinkles and worry lines into our cumulative written record.

Since then, Miss Kathie says she's ransacked Webster's luggage. We can't risk overlooking any new murder schemes. She's discovered yet another final chapter, a seventh draft of the *Love Slave* finale. "It would seem that I'm to be shot by an intruder next," she says, "when I interrupt him in the process of burgling my home."

But at last she's managed a counterattack: she's mailed this newest final chapter to her lawyer, sealed within a manila envelope, with the instructions that he should open it and read the contents should she meet a sudden, suspicious death. After that she informed the Webster of her actions. Of course he vehemently denied any plot; he protested and railed that he'd never written such a book. He insisted that he'd only ever loved her and had no intention to cause her harm. "But that's exactly," Miss Kathie says, "what I'd expected him to say, the evil cad."

Now, in the event Miss Kathie falls under an omnibus, bathes with an electric radio, feeds herself to grizzly bears, tumbles from a tall building, sheathes an assassin's sharp dagger with her heart or ingests cyanide—then **Webster Carlton Westward III** will never get to publish his terrible "lie-ography." Her lawyers will expose his ongoing plot. Instead of hitting any best-seller list, the Webster will go sit in the electric chair.

All the while, I drag the diamond's point to draw Miss Kathie's new gray hairs onto the mirror. I tap the glass to mark any new liver spots.

"I should be safe," Miss Kathie says, "from any homicidal burglars."

Under pressure, the mirror bends and distorts, stretching and warping my Miss Kathie's reflection. The glass feels that fragile, crisscrossed with so many flaws and scars.

Miss Kathie lifts her glass in a champagne toast to her reflected self, saying, "As Webb's ultimate punishment, I made him marry me. . . ."

The would-be assassin has now become her full-time, live-in love slave.

The bright-brown-eyed wonder will do her bidding, collect her dry cleaning, chauffeur her, scour her bathroom, run errands, wash her dishes, massage her feet and provide any specific oral-genital pleasure Miss Kathie deems necessary, until death do they part. And even then, it had best not be her death or the Webster will likely find himself arrested.

"But just to be on the safe side . . ." she says, and reaches to retrieve something off the stone shelf. From among the abandoned pill bottles and outdated cosmetics and contraceptives, Miss Kathie's hand closes around something she carries back to her fur coat pocket. She says, "Just in case . . ." and slips this new item, tinted red with rust, blue with oil, into her coat pocket.

It's a revolver.

ACT III, SCENE FOUR

Here we dissolve into yet another flashback. Let's see the casting office at **Monogram Pictures** or **Selig studios** along **Gower Street**, what everyone called "Poverty Row," or maybe the old **Central Casting** offices on **Sunset Boulevard**, where a crowd of would-be actresses mill about all day with their fingers crossed. These, the prettiest girls from across the world, voted **Miss Sweet Corn Queen** and **Cherry Blossom Princess**. A former reigning **Winter Carnival Angel**, a **Miss Bountiful Sea Harvest**. A pantheon of mythic goddesses made flesh and blood. **Miss Best Jitterbug**. A beauty migration, all of them vying for greater fame and glory. Among them, a couple of the girls draw your focus. One girl, her eyes are set too close together, her nose dwarfs her chin, her head rests squarely on her chest without any hint of an intervening neck.

The second young woman, waiting in the casting office,

cooling her heels . . . her eyes are the brightest amethyst purple. An almost supernatural violet.

In this flashback, we watch the ugly young woman, the plain woman, as she watches the lovely woman. The monstrous young woman, shoulders slumped, hands hanging all raw knuckled and gnawed fingernails, she spies on the young woman with the violet eyes. More important, the ugly woman watches the way in which the other people watch the lovely woman. The other actors seem stunned by those violet eyes. When the pretty one smiles, everyone watching her also smiles. Within moments of first seeing her, other people stand taller, pulling their bellies back to their spines. These queens and ladies and angels, their hands cease fidgeting. They adopt her same shoulders-back posture. Even their breathing slows to match that of the lovely girl. Upon seeing her, every woman seems to become a lesser version of this astonishing girl with violet eyes.

In this flashback, the ugly girl has almost given up hope. She's studied her craft with **Constance Collier** and **Guthrie McClintic** and **Margaret Webster**, yet she still can't find work. The homely girl does possess an innate, shrewd cunning; none of her gestures is ever without intention and motivation. In her underplaying, the ugly girl displays nothing short of brilliance. Even as she watches those present unconsciously mimic the lovely girl, the ugly one considers a plan. As a possible alternative to becoming an actress herself, perhaps the better strategy would be to join forces—combining her own skill and intelligence with the other girl's beauty. Between the two of them, they might yield one immortal motion picture star.

The homely girl might coach the pretty one, steer her into the best parts, protect her from dangerous shoals and entanglements of business and romance. The beastly girl can boast of no prominent cheekbones or Cupid's-bow mouth; still, such a bland face nurtures a nimble mind.

In contrast, beauty which evokes special favors and opens doors, such astounding eyes can cripple the brain behind them.

Counting backward, before the Webster was Paco, before him the senator. Before him the faggot chorus boy. Before that came the suicidal business tycoon, but even he wasn't her first husband. The first "was-band" was her high school sweetheart—Allan . . . *somebody*—some nobody. Her second was the sleazy photographer who snapped her picture and took it to a casting director; good riddance to him. Her third husband was an aspiring actor who's now selling real estate. None of those first three posed a threat.

While my position was never that of husband or spouse or partner, I was always far more important.

Oliver "Red" Drake, Esq., was another story. The founder of a steel smelting empire, only he possessed the resources to marry my Miss Kathie and give her a life at home, a passel of children, reduce her to the status of a **Gene Tierney** hausfrau . . . which is the Italian word for *loser*. Steel would buy her away from the larger world the way the **Grimaldi family** bought **Grace Kelly**, and I would be left with nothing to show for my effort.

Every husband had been a step forward in her career, but Oliver Drake represented a step forward in her personal life. By the time they'd met, Miss Kathie could no longer play the ingénue, which is Spanish for *slut*. The future meant scratching for character roles, featured cameos shot on location in obscure places. Instead of the glory of playing **Mrs. Little Lord Fauntleroy** or **Mrs. Wizard of Oz**, Miss Kathie would take billing in third place as the mother of **Captain Ahab** or the maiden aunt of **John the Baptist**.

Poised at that difficult fork in life, Miss Kathie was looking for an easier path.

It was so enormously selfish of her. The life's work of writers
and directors, artists and press agents had built this pedestal
she was tempted to abandon. There were larger things at
stake than love and peace. The independent, pioneering role
model for millions was leaving the stage. A legend seemed
about to retire. Thus the tycoon's apparent death by suicide
would preserve a cultural icon.

It was no difficult task to persuade several top film execu-
tives and directors to testify to Mr. Drake's depressed state
of mind. Some of Hollywood's biggest names swore that
Drake often spoke of ending his own life by cyanide. In that
manner, the film community was able to retain one of its
brightest investments.

In the flashback, we see the ugly girl wend her way closer
to the pretty one. With a studied, rehearsed nonchalance the
homely girl stumbles into contact with the beauty. Jostling
her, the clumsy beast says, "Gosh, I'm sorry. . . ."

The mob mills around them, that crowd of pretty anony-
mous faces. The **Hay Bale Queen**. The **Sweet Onion Princess**. Lovely, forgettable faces, born to flirt and fuck and die.

All those years and decades ago, the beauty smiles that
astonishing smile, saying, "My name's Kathie." She says,
"Really it's Katherine." Offering her hand, she says, "**Katherine Kenton**."

Every movie star is a slave to someone.

Even the masters serve their own masters.

As if in friendly greeting, the beast offers her own hand in
return, saying, "Pleased to meet you. I'm **Hazie Coogan**."

And the two young women join hands.

ACT III, SCENE FIVE

We slowly dissolve back to the present. The mise-en-scène: the daytime interior of a basement kitchen in the town house of **Katherine Kenton**; arranged along the upstage wall: an electric stove, an icebox, a door to the alleyway, a dusty window in said door. A narrow stairway leads up to the second floor. Still carved in the window glass, we see the heart from **Loverboy**'s arrival as a puppy, oh, scenes and scenes ago.

In the foreground, I sit on a white-painted kitchen chair with my feet propped on a similar white-painted table, my legs crossed at the ankle; my hands turn the pages of yet another screenplay. Open across my lap is a screenplay about **Lillian Hellman** starring **Lillian Hellman** written by **Lillian Hellman**.

Upstage, Miss Kathie's feet appear on the steps which descend from the second floor. Her pink slippers. The hem of her pink dressing gown. The gown flutters, revealing a flash of smooth thigh. Her hands appear, one clutching a ream of paper, her other hand clutching a wad of black fabric. Even before her face appears in the doorway, her voice calls, "Hazie . . ." Almost a shout, her voice says, "Someone telephoned me, just now, from the animal hospital."

On the page, Lilly Hellman runs faster than a speeding bullet. She's more powerful than a locomotive and able to leap tall buildings in a single bound.

Standing in the doorway, Miss Kathie holds the black fabric, the ream of papers. She says, "**Loverboy** did not die from eating chocolates . . ." and she throws the black fabric onto the kitchen table. There the fabric lies, creating a face of two empty eyes and an open mouth. It's a ski mask, identical to the one described in *Love Slave*, worn by the Yakuza assassin wielding the ice pick.

Miss Kathie says, "The very nice veterinarian explained to me that **Loverboy** was poisoned with cyanide. . . ."

Like so many others around here . . .

On the scripted page, Lilly Hellman parts the **Red Sea** and raises **Lazarus** from the dead.

"After that," she says, "I telephoned **Groucho Marx** and he says you never invited him to the funeral. . . ." Her violet eyes flashing, she says, "Neither did you invite **Joan Fontaine**, **Sterling Hayden** or **Frank Borzage**." Her dulcet voice rising, Miss Kathie says, "The only person you *did* invite was **Webster Carlton Westward III**."

She swings the ream of paper she holds rolled in her fist, swatting the pages against the black ski mask, making the kitchen table jump. Miss Kathie screams, "I found this mask, tucked away—*in your room*."

Such an accusation. My Miss Kathie says that I poisoned the Pekingese, then invited only the bright-eyed Webster to join us in the crypt so he could arrive bearing flowers at her moment of greatest emotional need. Throughout the past few months, while I've seemed to be warning her against the Webster, she insists that I've actually been aiding and abetting him. She claims I've been telling him when to arrive and how best to court her. After that, the Webster and myself, the two of us poisoned Terry by accident. She says the Webster and myself are plotting to kill her.

Bark, honk, cluck . . . **conspiracy**.

Oink, bray, tweet . . . **treachery**.

Moo, meow, whinny . . . **collusion most foul**.

On the screenplay page, Lilly Hellman turns water to wine. She heals the lepers. She spins filthy straw into the purest gold.

When my Miss Kathie pauses to take a breath, I tell her not to be ridiculous. Clearly, she's mistaken. I am not scheming with the Webster to murder her.

"Then how do you explain this?" she says, offering the pages in her hand. Printed along the top margin of each, a title. Typed there, it says, *Paragon: An Autobiography*. Authored by **Katherine Kenton**. As told to **Hazie Coogan**. Shaking her head, she says, "I did *not* write this. In fact, I *found* it tucked under *your* mattress. . . ."

The story of her life. Written in her name. By someone else.

Flipping past the title page, she looks at me, her violet eyes twitching between me and the manuscript she holds. Her pink dressing gown trembles. From the kitchen table, the empty ski mask stares up at the ceiling. " 'Chapter one,' " my Miss Kathie reads, " 'My life began in the truest and fullest sense the glorious day I first met my dearest friend, **Hazie Coogan**. . . .' "

ACT III, SCENE SIX

We continue with the audio bridge of **Katherine Kenton** reading from the manuscript of *Paragon*, "'. . . the glorious day I first met my dearest friend, **Hazie Coogan** . . .'"

Once more we see the two girls from the casting office. In a soft-focus montage of quick cuts, the ugly girl combs the long auburn hair of the pretty girl. Using a file, the ugly girl shapes the fingernails of the pretty girl, painting them with pink lacquer. Pursing her lips, the ugly girl blows air to dry the painted nails as if she were about to kiss the back of the pretty girl's hand.

Miss Kathie's movie-star voice continues, "'. . . living and playing together, cavorting amidst the adoring legions of our public . . .'"

In contrast, we see the girl with beady eyes and a beaky nose, watching as she tweezes the eyebrows above the violet eyes. The ugly girl kneels to scrape the dead skin off the pretty girl's heels using a pumice stone. Like a charwoman, the ugly girl rocks forward and back with the effort to scrub the pretty girl's bare back using sea salt and elbow grease.

My Miss Kathie's voice-over continues, " '. . . living and playing together, working seemingly endless hours, Hazie and I always supported and urged each other forward in this festive endeavor we so blithely refer to as life . . .' " She reads, " 'We lived so much like sisters that we even shared our wardrobes, wearing one another's shoes, exchanging even our undergarments with complete freedom. . . .' "

As the montage continues, the ugly girl sweats over an ironing board, pressing the lace and frills on a blouse, then giving it to the pretty girl. The ugly girl bends to lather and shave one of the pretty girl's long legs as it extends from a bathtub overflowing with luminous bubbles.

" 'I scratched her back,' " the voice of Miss Kathie reads, " 'and Hazie scratched mine. . . .' "

On-screen, the ugly girl delivers a breakfast tray to the pretty girl, who waits in bed.

" 'We made a special point to pamper each other,' " says the voice-over.

In the continuing ironic montage, the pretty girl puts a cigarette between her own lips, and the ugly girl leans forward to light it. The pretty girl drops a dirty towel on the floor, and the ugly girl picks it up for the laundry. The pretty girl sprawls in a chair, reading a screenplay, while the ugly girl vacuums the rug around her.

The voice of Miss Kathie reads, "And as our careers began to bear fruit, we both savored the rewards of success and fame. . . .' "

As the montage progresses, we see the ugly girl become a woman, still plain-looking, but aging, gaining weight, turning gray, while the pretty girl stays much the same, slender, her skin smooth, her hair a constant, rich auburn. In quick cuts, the pretty girl weds a man, then weds a new man, then weds a third man, then a fourth and fifth, while the ugly woman stands by, always burdened with luggage, shoulder bags, shopping bags.

In voice-over Miss Kathie says, " 'I owe everything I've become, really everything I've attained and achieved, to no one except **Hazie Coogan**. . . . ' "

As the ugly woman ages, we see her pretty counterpart laughing within a circle of reporters as they thrust radio microphones and photographers flash their cameras. The ugly woman always stands outside the spotlight, offstage in the wings, off-camera in the shadows, holding the pretty woman's fur coat.

Still reading from the manuscript of *Paragon*, Miss Kathie's voice says, " 'We shared the trials and the tears. We shared the fears and the greatest joys. Living together, shouldering the same burdens, we kept each other young. . . . ' "

In the montage, an adoring crowd, including **Calvin Coolidge**, **Joseph Pulitzer**, **Joan Blondell**, **Kurt Kreuger**, **Rudolph Valentino** and **F. Scott Fitzgerald**, looks on as the ugly woman places a birthday cake before the beauty. At that beat, we cut to the ugly one presenting another cake, obviously a year later. With a third quick cut, yet another cake is presented as **Lillian Gish**, **John Ford** and **Clark Gable** applaud and sing. With each successive cake, the ugly woman looks a bit older. The beauty does not. Every cake holds twenty-five blazing candles.

The reading continues, " 'Her job title was not that of secretary or acting coach, but **Hazie Coogan** deserves credit for all of my finest performances. She was not a spiritual guide or swami, but the best, truest adviser any person could ever treasure.' " Her voice rising, my Miss Kathie says, " 'If posterity finds continuing value in my films, humanity must also recognize the obligation of respect and gratitude owed to **Hazie Coogan**, the greatest, most talented friend for whom a simple player could ever ask.' "

With this statement, the beauty inhales deeply, surrounded by the beaming countenances of celebrities, everyone bathed in the flickering light from the birthday cake. Leaning forward, she blows out the birthday candles, and the festive scene drops to total and complete black. A silent, blank void.

Against this darkness, Miss Kathie's voice says, " 'The end.' "

ACT III, SCENE SEVEN

My life's work is complete.

For one final time we open in the crypt below the cathedral, where the veiled figure of a lone woman enters carrying yet another metal urn. She sets the urn alongside the urns of **Terrence Terry, Oliver "Red" Drake, Esq.,** and **Loverboy,** then lifts her black veil to reveal her face.

This woman dressed in widow's weeds is myself, **Hazie Coogan.** Unescorted.

Miss Kathie was mine. I invented her, time and time again. I rescued her.

After lighting a candle, I pop the cork on a bottle of champagne, one magnum still frothing, overflowing and alive in the company of so many dead soldiers. Into a dusty glass, milky with cobwebs, I pour a bubbling toast.

This is love. This is what love is. I've rescued her, who she was in the past and who she will be to the future. **Katherine**

Kenton will never be a demented old woman, consigned to the charity ward in some teaching hospital. No tabloid newspaper or movie magazine will ever snap the kind of ludicrous, decrepit photographs that humiliated **Joan Crawford** and **Bette Davis**. She will never sink into the raving insanity of **Vivien Leigh** or **Gene Tierney** or **Rita Hayworth** or **Frances Farmer**. Here would be a sympathetic ending, not a slow fade into drugs, a chaotic **Judy Garland** spiral into the arms of younger men, finally to be found dead sitting astride a rented toilet.

Hers would not be a slow, grinding death or a sad fading away. No, the legend of **Katherine Kenton** required an epic, romantic grand finale. Something drenched in glory and pathos. Now she would never be forgotten. I've given her that.

A dramatic exit—after a suitable third act.

I raise my glass and say, "Gesundheit." I drink a toast and pour another.

Please let me remove all doubt that **Webster Carlton Westward III** adored her. It was obvious the first time their eyes met down the length of that long-ago dinner party. He never wrote a word of *Love Slave,* despite how each draft was found in his luggage. No, all of those chapters were my doing, typed and tucked beneath his shirts, where I felt certain Miss Kathie would discover them. A woman torn between love and fear, it would be only a matter of time before she delivered a sealed copy to her lawyer or agent, where it would later implicate the Webster.

Forgive me for boasting, but mine was a perfect frame-up.

We intercut here with a tableau which the police discovered: Miss Kathie shot to death by a gun still gripped in the Webster's hand. It would appear that the pair slaughtered each other amid the candles and flowers of her boudoir. The result of a failed robbery attempt. Near her lies the corpse of Mr. Bright Brown Eyes wearing a black ski mask and shot by Miss Kathie's old gun, the rusted gun she'd retrieved from the crypt. Clutched in his hand, a pillowcase spills out pilfered praise, gold-plated, silver-plated trophies and awards. The symbolic keys to Midwestern cities. Honorary college degrees awarded to her for learning nothing.

If it is the case that love does survive death, then you may consider this to be a happy ending. Boy meets girl. Boy gets girl. Happily ever after or not.

In a **Samuel Goldwyn** touch, ham-handed as that final shot in his *Wuthering Heights*, we might include a quick flashback here. Just a quick reveal to show me shooting both the lovebirds in their bedroom, then staging the scene to suggest the burglary described in *Love Slave*. The surprise ending: that my role is not so much best friend or maid as villain. **Hazie Coogan** played the role of murderess. Perhaps in that last instant, Miss Kathie's violet eyes will register the full realization that she's been duped all along.

Slowly, we dissolve back to the Kenton crypt. . . . With the mirror propped in its customary place, positioned just so, I step to the lipstick X marked on the stone floor and superimpose my own face over the true face of my Miss Kathie. The lifetime of her scars and wrinkles, every distortion and defect she ever suffered, it's my own burden for the moment. The mirror itself sags with its collection of so many scratched insults. Every single one of Miss Kathie's faults and secrets.

The fur coat I'm wearing, it's her fur coat. My black veil, her veil. I reach into the slit of one pocket and retrieve the **Harry Winston** diamond ring. Kissing the ring, where it sits in the palm of my hand, I blow on it the way you would a kiss, and tumbling, thrown and flashing a low arc across the crypt, the diamond shatters the flawed reflection. What was an actual life story collapses into countless sparkling, glittering fragments. That single perfect image exploded into so many contradicting perspectives. The priceless diamond itself lost in this heap of so many worthless, dazzling glass shards.

Katherine Kenton will live for all time, preserved in the public mind, as permanent and lasting as silver-screen legends **Earl Oxford** and **House Peters**. Immortal as **Trixie Friganza**. Her face will be as familiar to future generations as the luminous, landmark face of **Tully Marshall**. Miss Kathie will continue to be worshiped, the way applauding audiences will forever worship **Roy D'Arcy**, **Brooks Benedict** and **Eulalie Jensen**.

From the shattered mirror, any true record of my Miss Kathie reduced to glittering slivers, from this the camera swings to focus on the newest urn. Coming closer and closer, we read the name engraved into the metal: *Katherine Ellen Kenton*.

To this I raise my glass.

ACT III, SCENE EIGHT

Act three, scene eight opens with **Lillian Hellman** throwing herself across the plush boudoir of **Katherine Kenton**, rocketing through the room and landing with her full weight upon the gun hand of a masked **Webster Carlton Westward III**. Lilly and the Webb struggle, throwing themselves about the bedroom, smashing chairs, lamps and bibelots in their raucous fight for survival. The muscles of Lilly's slim elegant arms strain to subdue the attacker. Her **Lili St. Cyr** lounging pajamas flapping and torn. Her **Valentino** hosiery devastated. Her elegant white teeth bite deep into the Webb's devious, scheming neck. The combatants tread on Lilly's fallen **Elsa Schiaparelli** hat while Katherine can only watch in abject horror, shrieking with doomed panic.

As in the opening scene, we dissolve to a long dinner table where Lilly sits, now regaling her fellow guests with the story of this struggle. The candlelight, the wood-paneled walls, the footmen. Lillian stops regaling long enough to draw one long drag on her cigarette, then blow the smoke over half the diners before she says, "If only I hadn't chosen to diet that week . . ." She taps cigarette ash onto her bread plate, shaking her head, saying, "My glorious, brilliant Katherine might still be alive. . . ."

Beyond her first few words, Lillian's talk becomes one of those jungle sound tracks one hears looping in the background of every **Tarzan** film, just tropical birds and howler monkeys repeating. *Bark, squeak, meow* . . . **Katherine Kenton.**

Oink, moo, tweet . . . **Webster Carlton Westward III.** A man who did nothing except fall deeply in love—passionately in love—he must now play the villain for the rest of this silly motion picture we call human history.

Miss Kathie's movie-star flesh has barely cooled, and already she's been absorbed into the Hellman mythos. Miss Lilly's own name-dropping form of **Tourette's syndrome.**

While the footmen pour wine and clear the sorbet dishes, Lillian's hands swim through the air, her cigarette trailing smoke, her fingernails clawing at an invisible burglar. In her dinner party story, Lilly continues to spar and struggle with the masked gunman. In their grappling, they fire a shot, which Hellman dramatizes by slapping her open palm on the table, making the silverware jump and the stemware ring together.

From my place, seated well below the salt, I merely listen to Lilly spin more gold into her own self-promoting dross. On my knee I bounce a jolly plump infant, one of the many orphans sent for Miss Kathie to review. Under my breath, I say a silent prayer that I might die after Lilly. To my left and right, from the head to the foot of the table, **Eva Le**

Gallienne, **Napier Alington**, **Blanche Bates**, **Jeanne Eagels**, we all say the same prayer. **George Jean Nathan** of *Smart Set* magazine draws a fountain pen from his chest pocket and scribbles notes on a napkin. **Edwin Schallert** of the *Los Angeles Times* spies him, taking notes about Nathan's notes. **Bertram Block** jots notes about Schallert's notes about Nathan's notes.

The possibility of dying before **Lillian Hellman** . . . dying and becoming merely fodder for Lilly's mouth. A person's entire life and reputation reduced to some golem, a Frankenstein's monster Miss Hellman can reanimate and manipulate to do her bidding. That would be a fate worse than death, to spend eternity in harness, serving as Lilly Hellman's zombie, brought back to life at dinner parties. On radio shows and in Hellman's autobiographies.

It was **Walter Winchell** who once said, "After any dinner with Lilly Hellman, you don't crave dessert and coffee—what you really need is the antidote."

Even the most illustrious names, once they're dead long enough, are reduced to silly animal sounds. *Grunt, bark, bray* . . . **Ford Madox Ford** . . . **Miriam Hopkins** . . . **Randle Ayrton**.

Seated to my right, **Charlie McCarthy** congratulates me on the success of my book. As of this week, *Paragon* has been at number one on the *New York Times* best-seller list for twenty-eight weeks.

Seated across the table, **Madeleine Carroll** inquires in that rich British accent of hers, asking the name of the child in my lap.

In response, I explain how this tiny foundling had been adopted by Miss Kathie, and now I have become its legal guardian. I've inherited the town house, the rights to

Paragon, all of the investments and this child, who sputters and smiles, a perfect blond angel. Its name, I explain, is **Norma Jean Baker**.

No, none of us seem so very real.

We're only supporting characters in the lives of each other.

Any real truth, any precious fact will always be lost in a mountain of shattered make-believe.

I signal, and a footman pours more wine. In my mind, I'm already crafting a story wherein **Lillian Hellman** thrashes and fusses and plays the boring, egomaniacal fool. **Lillian Hellman** plays the villain the way Webster plays the villain. In my own story of tonight, this dinner party, I'll be cool and collected and right. I shall say the perfect rejoinder. I will play the hero.

Please promise you did *NOT* hear this from me.

Cut. Print it. Roll credits.

(end)

Chuck Palahniuk's ten previous novels are the best-selling *Pygmy, Snuff, Rant, Haunted, Lullaby, Diary, Choke*—which has been made into a film by director Clark Gregg, starring Sam Rockwell and Anjelica Huston—*Survivor, Invisible Monsters,* and *Fight Club,* which was made into a film by director David Fincher. He is also the author of the nonfiction profile of Portland, Oregon, *Fugitives and Refugees,* published as part of the Crown Journeys series, and the nonfiction collection *Stranger Than Fiction.* He lives in the Pacific Northwest.